PLAYBOY

Royal Bastards MC: Sacramento
Book 1

Wall Street Journal & USA Today Bestselling Author
Winter Travers

Much love!

D1527761

For questions or comments about this book, please contact the author at winter@wintertravers.com

6

ROYAL BASTARDS MC SERIES

Erin Trejo: *Blood Lust*
Chelle C Craze & Eli Abbott: *Bad Like Me*
K Webster: *Koyn*
Esther E. Schmidt: *Petros*
Elizabeth Knox: *Bet On Me*
Glenna Maynard: *Lady & the Biker*
Madison Faye: *Filthy Bastard*
CM Genovese: *Frozen Rain*
J. Lynn Lombard: *Blayze's Inferno*
Crimson Syn: *Inked In Vengeance*
B.B. Blaque: *Rotten Apple*
Addison Jane: *Her Ransom*
Izzy Sweet * Sean Moriarty: *Broken Wings*
Nikki Landis: *Ridin' For Hell*
KL Ramsey: *Savage Heat*
M.Merin: *Axel*
Sapphire Knight: *Bastard*
Bink Cummings: *Switch Burn*
Winter Travers: *Playboy*
Linny Lawless: *The Heavy Crown*
Jax Hart: *Desert King*
Elle Boon: *Royally Broken*
Kristine Allen: *Voodoo*
Ker Dukey: *Animal*
KE Osborn: *Defining Darkness*
Shannon Youngblood: *Silver & Lace*

Royal Bastards MC Facebook Group -
https://www.facebook.com/groups/royalbastardsmc/
Website- https://www.royalbastardsmc.com/

Black Belt Knockout

Nitro Crew Series
Burndown
Holeshot
Redlight
Shutdown

Sweet Love Novellas
Sweet Burn
Five Alarm Donuts

Stand Alone Novellas
Kissing the Bad Boy
Daddin' Ain't Easy
Silas: A Scrooged Christmas
Wanting More
Mama Didn't Raise No Fool

Table of Contents

Chapter One

Playboy

Just another Saturday?

"Where are you going?"

I dropped my cigarette to the gravel and snuffed it out with the toe of my boot. "Bed."

Jet inhaled deep on his cigarette. "Alone or you got company joining you?" he wheezed before blowing out a plume of smoke.

"Right now, alone, but we both know that can change from here to my bedroom door."

It was early Saturday morning at the Sacramento Skinz strip club, and I was ready to call it a night. Most of the dancers were offstage and done for the evening which meant I was going to have my pick of the girls to warm my bed tonight.

"Barracuda talk to you?"

I nodded. "Tried to avoid him, but he tracked me down."

"That means you're in charge of the new weekend muscle?"

That was exactly what it meant. "He

tried to shine it up by saying I was the head of security, but we all fucking know it means I'm the one throwing out drunk assholes Friday and Saturday nights."

Jet chuckled. "Well, at least you have a week to get used to it."

"I'd rather Barracuda work out whatever shit is going on with the security company than have the club do security."

"Hey, just think of it like when the club first opened Skinz. We rotated nights, and it worked."

That was before the club became so well known. Now, with Skinz being popular, there were easily one hundred and fifty people in the club at any time. When there was an event going like jello wrestling or bubble parties, that number almost tripled.

"Well, I can handle it for a little bit, but I fucking hope Barracuda is looking for a new security company."

"You'll have your first shot at the girls if you're working security."

I rolled my eyes. I had first shot at the girls either way. I wasn't called Playboy for nothing. "I'll catch ya later, Jet."

I opened the door to the club, and the loud thumping of the bass hit me along with the smell of whiskey and cheap perfume. God knew these girls made a shit-ton of money, but it seemed like they all wore the same fucking overly sweet scent.

Normally, I knew what girl I wanted. They seemed to rotate through with barely any lasting more than a few nights. Tonight, it was different.

I made my way through the back of the club, my eyes darting to the changing room for the girls.

"You need some company tonight, Playboy?"

My gaze fell on Raine. She waltzed over to the door and leaned against the frame.

"What do you have in mind, sugar?"

She shrugged and draped her arm over her head. "Whatever you want, baby."

Raine was one of the first girls I had slept with when the strip club opened, and she had been clamoring to get back into my bed since. "Don't you think Tank and Rebel will mind me honing in on you?"

She reached out and trailed a finger down my chest. "You know they won't mind. Hell, Tank would probably join us."

That was true, but it wasn't anything I was interested in. "Maybe another time, Raine." She should have gotten the hint by now that I wasn't interested in her anymore, but obviously, she hadn't clued into it yet. Adding Tank into the equation was her latest ploy. *Hard pass.*

"We all know you don't want to be alone tonight, Playboy."

I gently grabbed her hand and dropped it. "Who said I was going to be alone?"

She scoffed and pushed off the doorframe. "Waste of my damn time," she mumbled under her breath.

My eyes darted around the room filled with loads of mirrors, half naked women, and a plume of hairspray that hung in the air. Nothing held my attention for more than a second. "Have a good night, ladies," I called.

I made my way down the hallway and pushed into the main room with a nod to one of the prospects who was guarding the door from the dressing rooms into the club.

Next Saturday, I would be one of the poor saps making sure the drunks don't get too handsy and try to run back to the girls when they get off stage. I was going to make sure the prospects took all the shit duties, and I can hopefully find a corner to sit in and just keep an eye on everything.

Prospects were supposed to have the shit jobs. I had been down the prospect path, and I had no intention of heading back down it even if Barracuda told me to do it.

Vivid Vanessa was on the stage, and she had the attention of every dick in the room. The one girl who had yet to look my way, and I was strangely okay with it. She had moves like no other on the pole, but something made me take a step back from pursuing her. She seemed like she would want a whole hell of a lot more than I had to offer. She didn't mess with any of the club guys, and she just had a classy air about her.

I was at the door when a petite hand grabbed my arm. "Looking for company tonight, Playboy?"

Bray. I looked her up and down and smiled. "Maybe, but you might want to put on some more clothes. It's pretty chilly on the back of my bike."

Bray flitted her long lashes. "Give me ten minutes? I need to count my drawer and change."

I nodded. "Meet me at my bike." Bray wasn't exactly what I was looking for, but she would keep my bed warm for a bit.

"Ten minutes," she promised. She turned on her heels toward the bar, and I pushed open the door to the outside.

My bike was in the front row and off to the right. Four other bikes of club members stood parked by mine, and there were about twenty other cars in the lot. My phone buzzed in my pocket, and I pulled it up to my ear.

"'Sup?"

"Where you at?" Six-Gun asked.

I sat down on my bike and pulled my keys out of my pocket. "Just leaving the club."

"You got someone here looking for you."

I stuck the key in the ignition but didn't turn it. "Who is it?"

"A chick."

That wasn't really surprising. "You wanna be a little bit more specific than that?"

"Brown hair. Dressed like a fucking librarian. Possibly hot if she took off the glasses and her eyes stopped darting around like a scared animal."

I knocked up the kick stand. "She got a name?" I had no idea who the hell Six-Gun was talking about, but I was fucking intrigued.

"Won't tell me. I asked her twice, but all she did was shake her head."

"She's still there?"

"That's why I fucking called you, brother. She's here, and she wants to talk to you."

I glanced over my shoulder toward the club. "I'll be there in five minutes." I shoved the phone in my pocket and started up the bike.

Bray was going to have to find someone else to keep her warm tonight.

*

Chapter Two

Raelyn

A chiseled god named Playboy…

This was a mistake.

This was so stupid.

What in the hell was I doing?

I rubbed my sweaty palms on my jeans and closed my eyes.

Just figure out where Billie Jean is and get the hell out of here, Raelyn. That was all I needed to do.

The only kink in that was the person I wanted to talk to wasn't here.

"He should be here in a couple of minutes." My head snapped up. The guy who I had been talking to came back down the hallway he had wandered to with his phone in his hand. "He's on the way back from the club. You wanna wait here or in his room?"

I opened my mouth to answer, but I didn't actually have one. I really wanted to run out of here and never look back, but this was my last resort. I didn't know who else to ask for help.

The guy shook his head and chuckled. "Tell you what. Playboy normally comes in the back door. Give it ten minutes and then go knock on his door, yeah?"

I blinked and nodded. "Uh, if you think that's best."

The guy shook his head. "I think it's best for you, doll. You look like you're about to puke all over the floor."

I gulped and tried to quell my rolling stomach. "I'm fine. I just need to talk to Playboy."

The guy looked me up and down. "You ain't his type, doll. You sure it's Playboy you're looking for?"

That was the name Billie Jean had mentioned. She said Playboy had bailed her out of a couple of dicey situations before. I had a feeling she was in a dicey situation right now, and Playboy needed to help *me* bail her out. I nodded again. "I need to talk to Playboy."

The guy tipped his head to the side. "And you can't tell me your name?"

I looked around the clubhouse. I had never been inside an MC clubhouse before, and the only knowledge I had about them was from TV shows. A bar took up the whole length of one wall, and there were ten stools in front of it. There was a large pool table in the center of the space, and six round tables with chairs sat scattered around the room. A large TV hung on the wall, and two guys were sitting on a large leather couch watching some action movie.

When I had knocked on the front door, no one had answered, and I stood out there for ten minutes before I gathered enough courage to try the door handle. I was sort of surprised when it opened easily, but the three guys who were on the other side of the door looked even more surprised.

The two on the couch hadn't talked to me, but I could feel them watching me the whole time. The guy who had been talking to me asked me my name, but I never told him.

"Raelyn," I croaked. "My name is Raelyn."

The guy nodded. "Six-Gun."

I tipped my head to the side and tried to figure out what that meant. "Uh, come again?" What an odd thing to say after someone told you their name.

"The name is Six-Gun, doll."

"Oh," I gasped. I was dumb and forgot that most bikers didn't go by their real names. Hence why I was looking for a guy called Playboy. "That's, uh, sweet?"

Jesus. I pressed my palm to my forehead and wished I had the power to rewind time and take back the word "sweet." *How is the name Six-Gun sweet, Raelyn?*

"Uh, never been called that before, but I guess I'll take it." Six-Gun twisted around and looked down the hallway he had just walked from. "Sounds like Playboy is back. You can head back to his room."

That was a hell of a lot faster than ten minutes. I had walked in ready to ask Playboy for help, but when he wasn't here right away, I retreated back to being a coward who wasn't ready to talk to him. "It's only been three minutes." If that. Did the guy break the speed of the light to get here?

"You can either go back there on your own terms or I can guarantee he'll be out here in a minute trying to figure out what you want."

Well. This was a dilemma. I could wait for him or I could go back there. "Uh, which door is his?"

Yeah, I would much rather talk to him without three other guys listening.

"Head down the hallway, hang a left, and he's the second door on the left."

I nodded stiffly and willed my feet to move. My legs shifted woodenly, and I'm sure I looked like a nutcracker walking toward Playboy's room.

I heard muffled laughter, but I didn't look back at Six-Gun. If I did, I was likely to make a run for the front door. I made it to the end of the hallway and turned to the left. I passed the first door on the left and then stopped in front of the second door.

I raised my fist, knocked lightly on the door, and waited.

Three seconds passed before the door swung open and my eyes fell on the most beautiful rugged man I had ever seen. Normally, rugged and beautiful didn't go together, but those were the two exact words I would use to describe Playboy.

Beautiful.

Rugged.

His eyes traveled over me, but mine were doing the same to him.

He wasn't seeing much by looking at me, but I was getting one heck of an eye full.

Distressed jeans encased his legs, and black boots adorned his feet. His black shirt pulled taut across his chest, and the left sleeve was rolled up with what I assumed was a pack of cigarettes wrapped in it.

Dark ink swirled around his forearm and traveled up into his sleeve, and my fingers itched to pull up the fabric to see the tattoo. His arms were muscled and tanned from being out in the sun, and his neck showed another hit of ink. I wondered if it connected to the ink on his arm. Tattoos had never really been my thing, but seeing Playboy made me rethink my opposition to them.

His jawline looked like it had been chiseled from stone and sprinkled with stubble.

Mustache.

The man had a mustache, and I had never seen something sexier in my life. My nether regions gave a slight ache at the thought of feeling the stubbly hair between my legs.

Focus, Raelyn. I hadn't even spoken one word to the guy, and I was already imaging what his mouth would feel like on me. If this was any indication, I could see why he got the road name of Playboy.

"I heard you were looking for me, darlin'."

My eyes snapped to his, and I realized he had ended his perusal of me way before I had finished gaping at him. "I, uh, well, yeah."

Real smooth. From the moment I had left my house and driven to the clubhouse, I had been confident and determined to convince Playboy to help me. I wasn't going to take no for an answer. Now, it seemed like I couldn't string a complete and coherent sentence together.

"I think you're at a little bit of an advantage seeing as you know my name but I don't have a clue what yours is."

Even his voice was rugged and beautiful. *How?* How was that freaking possible? And, of course he wouldn't know my name, let alone even know I existed. Playboy was the type of man who would never, in a million years, look my way, let alone know my name.

"Uh, Raelyn. Well, some people call me Rae, but I'm Raelyn. You can call me Raelyn. Raelyn." He could also call me Rain Man. I cringed and turned to look back down the hallway. I took a deep breath and forced my gaze to return to Playboy. "My name is Raelyn, and I need to talk to you." There, that was what I intended to say all along. I needed the past thirty seconds to be erased so I could start over.

"Don't know how much we have to talk about when I've never met you before, darlin'."

The endearment rolled off his lips too easily, and I knew he wasn't calling me anything special.

"If you let me in, I can explain."

He eyed me closely. "Even if you explain, I don't know what the hell you think I can do for you."

I knew getting through the door was going to be the hardest part of all of this. His name might have been Playboy, and he may have been good with the ladies, but did that

mean he let just anyone into his room?
Obviously not. "It's about Billie Jean."

He tipped his head to the side. "How do
you know Billie Jean?"

It was a valid question. Anyone who
knew Billie Jean and then met me would
wonder how the hell we even knew each other.
Billie Jean had a blunt chin-length haircut that
was ever changing colors. She loved wearing
anything leather, and she had a panache for
piercings. It didn't matter where they were, she
loved them. The only holes that were man-made
on me were in my ears. My hair was mousey
brown, and I favored wearing jeans and
sweatshirts. Exact opposites.

"I've known her for a while."

That was a slight understatement. We
were twins. I had known her every second of
my life. That was awhile, right?

"You didn't answer my question."

I folded my arms over my chest. "I'll
tell you if you let me in."

Whether being her sister was going to
be in my favor or not was still to be seen. She
talked about Playboy helping her out, but I half
wondered if she exaggerated everything she had
told me. Billie Jean had a knack of spinning an
interesting story that always made you wonder
the validity of what she said. The bones of the

story were true, but she always put on flair to make it exciting.

"You're not her girlfriend."

I wrinkled my nose. "No, I'm not," I stated plainly.

Billie Jean had a few girlfriends she rotated through, but I obviously wasn't one of them. *Hello, twins.* I hoped for the day that she would find the girl she wanted to actually stay with, but now I was worried about whether she would ever get that chance or if she was dead somewhere.

Playboy mumbled and stepped to the side. "I might regret this."

He wasn't going to. I slipped into the room and tried to ignore the fact that my breasts brushed against his arm. *Focus, Raelyn.* "I promise you won't."

"You're not the first woman to tell me that." He closed the door and turned to me.

I stood next to his bed and tried to not cower like a lost little girl. It wasn't working.

My hands fidgeted at my sides with the seam of my jeans, and I bit my lip. Not exactly confident and sure looking.

"So, how do you know Billie Jean?"

I cleared my throat. "Uh, how do you know Billie Jean?" Yeah, I was an idiot. Answer a question with a question. *Facepalm.*

Playboy shook his head and chuckled. He pulled the pack cigarettes out of his sleeve and tapped one out. He stuck it in the corner of his mouth and tossed the pack on the dresser next to the bed. "Can't believe I left Bray at the club for this."

Hmph. I clamped my mouth shut to not ask who Bray was. *Not my business.* "Billie Jean is my sister. We're twins. And you can't smoke in here." Yeah, I had gone from being meek and mild to telling Playboy he couldn't smoke in his own room. I needed to get a damn grasp on what the heck I was doing.

Play pulled a lighter out of his pocket and rolled his thumb over the wheelie thing to spark it. He held it to the cigarette and inhaled deep. He tossed the lighter in the direction of the pack of cigarettes and blew out a plume of smoke. "You really think I'm going to believe that you and Billie Jean are related?"

I waved my hand in front of my face to diffuse the smoke and pulled my phone out of my pocket. I had expected this. It really was hard to believe that Billie Jean and I shared blood. I pulled up my first piece of photographic evidence. "This was us, senior year."

I held the phone up in his direction. The photo was from almost eight years ago, but you could see the resemblance between Billie Jean and me. We obviously weren't identical twins. Billie Jean was slender and had a dancer's build. I, on the other hand, looked more like a plump couch potato.

Playboy stepped toward me and squinted at the picture. "That doesn't even look like Billie Jean."

I rolled my eyes and turned the phone back to me. "That's because Billie Jean hadn't found her love for tattoos and piercings yet," I grumbled. I was going to have to pull out some more recent ones if I really wanted to convince him. "Last Halloween."

It was a great picture of Billie Jean, but it wasn't exactly very flattering of me. We had gone as a group for Halloween as the Village People. I was the only one out of the group who took it very literally and dressed up with mustache and authentic *manly* police uniform. Billie Jean and her four friends from the club had dressed up as a sexy construction worker, sailor, cowboy, biker, and Indian. Can you guess which one of us went home alone that night?

Playboy squinted hard at the photo. "Is that a mustache?"

I snatched the phone away and scowled. "I didn't connect the Village People as being sexy, okay?" I shoved my phone back in my pocket and realized Playboy was standing right in front of me. "Now, can we move on from the fact that Billie Jean and I are related?"

Playboy again just stared at me. He inhaled on his cigarette. "So you're related to one of the girls from the club. Still don't understand what you want from me."

"I can't find Billie Jean."

"She works tonight?"

I shook my head. "I haven't been able to talk to her for the past four days."

Playboy moved to the long dresser and tapped his cigarette in the ashtray. "I haven't seen her."

"I'm not asking if you've seen her. I know something happened to her, and I need your help to find her." Might as well get straight to the point. I was a duck out of water in Billie Jean's world. We may have been sisters, but that didn't mean I traveled in the same circles that she did.

"How do you know something happened to her?"

"Because I just know."

Call it twin intuition or whatever. Billie Jean and I talked every day. *Everyday*. Even if she was running out the door to work and I was tucking myself into bed, Billie Jean and I talked all of the time.

"And why am I supposed to help you?"

The next hurdle I knew I was going to face. I got in the door, and now, I needed to convince Playboy to help me. There really wasn't much I had to offer besides two things.

I reached into my back pocket and pulled out a wad of cash. "I've got four thousand dollars."

Playboy laughed. "So do I, darlin'." He nodded to the bedside table. "Three in there and five in the dresser. You're offering something I already have."

I thought that might be a snag in my plan. Granted, I had hoped like hell I wouldn't have to offer the next thing. "Four thousand dollars…and I'll do anything you want."

Playboy quirked his eyebrow, and a smirk spread across his lips. "Now we're talking."

I had awoken something inside of Playboy, and I prayed to God I was woman enough to follow through with my proposition.

*

Chapter Three

Playboy

A deal with a Bastard...

She was different.

So fucking different.

The thing that got me and I couldn't take my mind off of were her fucking eyes.

Vivid, frosty blue. They pierced through me, and I felt she could see all my scars and doubts. I was good at putting on a confident façade, but Raelyn seemed to be the one who could break through with her innocence and awkward confidence.

She opened her mouth, but no words came out.

I was open to whatever she had in mind if it meant she would stay in my room for a bit longer. I'd had instant attraction before, but it usually died off as soon as it happened. Two minutes with Raelyn and I wanted to know a whole hell of a lot more than just what she would feel like beneath me.

"I need help to find Billie Jean," she cleared her throat, "and I'm willing to do whatever I need to for you to help me. Please."

She tucked the money back in her pocket and adjusted the glasses on her face.

How in the hell was Billie Jean related to this chick? And to find out she was her twin sister. That was fucking mind-blowing.

Billie Jean had worked at Skinz for two years as a waitress, and never, in a million years, would I have imagined this woman being her sister. Billie Jean was forward and a bit crass. Two things that worked in your favor when you were a waitress at a strip club.

Looking at Raelyn, I had to wonder if she had ever stepped foot in a strip club. She was all soft and innocent looking. The fact she actually had the balls to walk into the clubhouse was pretty fucking astonishing.

"What makes you think Billie Jean is actually missing and not just off on a bender with her latest girlfriend?" I didn't know a ton about Billie Jean, but I had bailed her out of a pinch at the club a time or two. Drunk guys watching naked chicks they couldn't touch sometimes made situations where they thought they can lay hands on the waitresses.

"Because I haven't heard from her since Tuesday night. She called me right before she went to work that night, and since then, I haven't heard a word from her."

That really wasn't that long to me. Hell, Mom and Dad hadn't heard from me in probably a month. Four days? That was fucking nothing. "I'm sure she'll turn up."

Raelyn shook her head. "I know something happened to her, Playboy."

My name rolling off her tongue sounded foreign. I could tell it was a word she had never spoken out loud before. At least, not before tonight. I folded my arms over my chest. "I don't get why you're knocking down my door for help. I'm not anyone's hero, Raelyn."

That couldn't be any closer to the truth. I was here on the Earth for a good time and that was it.

"I don't know what else to do." Raelyn paced back and forth and ran her fingers through her hair. "I called all of Billie Jean's friends and even went to the club to talk to the ones I didn't have numbers for."

"Wait, wait," I interrupted. "You went to Skinz?"

Why did I have an urge to yell at Raelyn for putting herself in risk of getting hurt?

She nodded. "I only went inside for two minutes, though. I left because it was crowded. I just waited 'til her friends came out, and then, I asked them if they had heard from her."

34

Jesus. The parking lot of Skinz was not the type of place Raelyn should have been hanging out. "When were you at the club?"

"Last night. I was hoping to see you there, but then I realized I didn't know what you looked like so I stuck with trying to talk to her friends." Raelyn stopped pacing and turned to me. "None of them had seen her since her shift on Tuesday. They all said she seemed fine when she left at two-thirty and then, poof, she's gone."

"Why haven't you gone to the police?" To me, that seemed like the first thing a girl like Raelyn would have done. Hanging out in strip club parking lots and walking into an MC clubhouse seemed a little out of the norm for her.

"Because all I can tell them is, I have a feeling she's missing, but I have no actual proof that she is. And…adding in the facts that she works at a strip club and she's been on the wrong side of the law a couple of times even though she always came out with a clean record."

She could be right about that. Even I had said at first that she was just out on a bender. "Call her."

Raelyn rolled her eyes but pulled out her phone. "I've called her at least a hundred times, Playboy. You think she is going to answer now that you're here?"

It was a possibility, but that wasn't why I wanted her to call Billie Jean.

Raelyn swiped a couple of times on her phone and then put it on speaker. It rang seven times, and then, it went to voicemail. Raelyn ended the call and shoved it back in her pocket. "She doesn't answer."

"But it rings," I pointed out. "That means her phone isn't dead. If she's been gone for four days, she's had to have charged her phone at some point."

"Or someone stole her phone and knows not to answer when I call."

Again, that was a possibility. "Or she's out having the time of her life and doesn't feel like answering her phone." God knew there were days like that for me.

"She's not," Raelyn said through clenched teeth. "Something is wrong, and I need your help."

I sat down on the edge of the bed, folded my arms over my chest, and looked up at Raelyn. "I don't know how I'm going to help you."

"You know people, and you've helped Billie Jean before," she insisted.

"I don't know what kind of people you think I run with, and I've helped her when guys get handsy at the club. Not when she's fucking missing."

Raelyn stepped toward me. "Four grand, you get whatever you want from me, and you help me find Billie Jean."

I was going to let her proposition slide before because I didn't think she really meant it, but she said it again. Women like Raelyn didn't know the types of things I liked to do to women. "I don't think you know just what you're offering me."

She took another step toward me. "I'm not some dumb girl, Playboy. Your name alone tells me what you'll want from me."

"What happens if I can't find Billie Jean?" I had no fucking clue where to start looking for her, and I didn't want to get Raelyn's hopes up at all. "I know her from the club and have never hung out with her outside of there."

"Just give me a week. If you don't figure anything out, I'll disappear and you'll never see me again," she pleaded. She took another step toward me and bumped into my knees. "Please."

"Raelyn," I spoke softly. "You're offering me a lot for maybe not finding your sister at all."

She stared at me and didn't speak. Her eyes begged me, and there was no way in hell I was going to tell her no. And, I was a ruthless bastard anyway. Offering herself up to me twice was one more time than necessary. "Tell me everything you know."

"Does that mean you are going to help me?" she asked, hopeful.

My gaze connected with hers. "One week. I'm not making any promises that I'll find anything, but I'll do what I can." I wasn't really offering her much. My connections could get me only so far and who was to say that they would know anything about Billie Jean. "You can keep your money, though."

She tipped her head to the side. "But…" she trailed off.

"Keep your money." I was far more interested in the other thing she had offered me, except I wasn't going to take her until she wanted me to. I was a savage, but I wasn't an asshole. "I'll collect on the other part of your offer later."

Her face fell, and I think she expected me to take her right then and there. "Oh, okay."

I scrubbed my hands down my face and resisted the urge to wipe the frown off her face with a kiss to seal the deal. I held my hand out to her. "Shake on it."

She looked at my hand. "Shake?"

Yeah, she totally thought I was going to take my part of the deal right then and there. "Yeah, darlin'."

She wrinkled her nose. "It's Raelyn."

I shook my head. "I know. Remember, you told me about five times when we first met."

She rolled her eyes and put her hand in mine. "I'd like to never be reminded of our first meeting. Can we add that into the deal?"

I gently squeezed her small hand and shook it. "Adding to the deal after we agreed on it?" I chuckled.

She watched our hands clasped together. "It's a small adjustment."

"I might need something more from you, then."

Her eyes darted up to mine. "Like?"

I shrugged. "You'll find out eventually."

"That doesn't exactly seem fair," she retorted.

"You just made a deal with a Royal Bastard, darlin'. Do you really think we got our name for being fair?"

She tried to yank her hand from mine, but I squeezed it tighter and tugged her to me. "Playboy," she gasped.

I leaned toward her and pulled her hand to my chest. "Know one thing, darlin'. I get to do whatever I want to you, but you're going to be wanting it just as much as I am."

A gasp escaped her lips, and her eyes widened.

She wanted me.

Raelyn was something I never had before.

She was the type of girl who would never look my way, but I had her where I wanted her, and you could bet your ass I was going to take everything I craved.

Find her sister and then make Raelyn mine.

*

Chapter Four

Raelyn

Was this what I wanted?

"Wanna go out for drinks?"

I shut down my computer and looked up at Leona. "It's Monday."

"Uh, that's a pretty damn good reason to go get a drink," she laughed. "I'm pretty sure you were the one who was ready to throw the phone through the window when the shipment of lumber was delayed four days to the building site."

That was the damn truth. Most of the time, my job was pretty mindless and easy, but when delayed shipments happened, they were a wrench in a normally well-oiled machine. "I think I'm just gonna head home."

It had been almost a week since I had last heard from Billie Jean, and it was weighing heavily on me that something horrible had happened to her.

Playboy had taken my number after we shook hands and then sent me on my way. He promised he would call me if he found out anything, but so far, nothing from him. I had been a dumbass and not taken his number so I was basically sitting around waiting for any news from him. I could always go to the clubhouse and try to find him again, but I wasn't going to. At least, not yet.

"Come one, Raelyn," Leona whined. "We're two sexy women who need to get out and have a drink."

"Speak for yourself," I laughed. "I'm far from sexy, and all I want to do is go home, slip my shoes off, and eat half a frozen pizza." Hell, who was I kidding? I was totally going to eat the whole damn thing. "Raincheck on the drink." I was also going to worry myself sick waiting to hear from Playboy.

"Fine," Leona grumbled. "But I'm holding you to that raincheck, though."

I grabbed my purse and stood. I hitched it over my shoulder and grabbed my keys off the desk. "Next Monday. You and me."

Hopefully by then, Billie Jean would be back home, and everything would go back to normal.

Two minutes later, I was in my car and headed home. I stopped by the local pizza place for a large pie after I decided to splurge and get a fresh pizza instead of frozen.

My mind was on Billie Jean when I turned onto my street, and I almost crapped myself when my driveway came into view and

Playboy was sitting on his bike in front of my house. My heart leapt, and I couldn't decide if it was a good sign or not. Maybe he had found Billie Jean and he had brought her home. Maybe he had found Billie Jean but she was dead.

I shook my head. *No, I can't think like that.* I pulled into my driveway and kept my eye on my rearview mirror.

Playboy sat on his bike, a cigarette hanging from his mouth, and his eyes were on my car.

Smoking was gross, and I hated the smell of it.

Except when Playboy did it. Granted, I still hated the smell of it, but there was something mesmerizing about it when it was that man. I watched him while he finished the cigarette and then he tossed it on the ground. He threw his leg over the bike and stood. He started up the driveway, and I finally got into motion.

I grabbed my purse from the passenger side seat and pushed open my door.

Playboy was walking up my driveway, and my heart felt like it was about to beat out of my chest. He could be approaching to give me horrible news about Billie Jean, but I couldn't help but feel excited to see him again.

I slipped out of the car and turned toward him. "Uh, hey there," I called. I hitched my purse over my shoulder and tried not to cringe after my lame hello.

"Darlin'," he rumbled.

I still wasn't a fan of being called *darlin'*, even though it sounded so smooth rolling off his tongue. "I, uh, didn't know you were coming by."

Obviously. I really needed to just keep my mouth shut and let Playboy take the lead. He was the one who had shown up at my house, so he could be the one to do the talking. I had been ready to veg out in front of the TV and eat a whole pizza.

Playboy stopped in front of me, and his eyes traveled over my body. "Thought I would come by. Talk."

I nodded dumbly. Talk about my sister being dead in a ditch or talk about the fact he had found her? "We can do that." I nodded to the backseat. "I grabbed a pizza on the way home. You like pizza?"

Ugh. I asked Playboy if he liked pizza as if he was a three-year-old. *Kill. Me. Now.*

A smirk spread across his lips. "I'm a single guy who doesn't cook. Yeah, I like pizza." He looked in the back seat. "And I especially like Dough's Pizza."

He would have to be dead to not like Dough's. It was the best pizza within two hundred miles.

He opened the backdoor of the car and grabbed the box of pizza. "Breadsticks?" he asked as he held up the white bag that had a huge grease spot on it.

"Can't have pizza without breadsticks," I mumbled. That was a hard rule I lived by. If you were going to splurge and have pizza, you might as well as go all the way and get the breadsticks, too. I closed my door and headed toward the house. "Follow me," I called.

I didn't look over my shoulder, but I could feel Playboy following me closely.

"Nice place."

I pulled my keys out of my purse and stuck the key into the lock. "Uh, thanks. I like it."

More like I loved it. I had worked my ass off for a year to save enough for a down payment. It was my first house, and I planned on living here for a damn long time. It was big enough to grow into, but not so big that I got lost with it just being myself right now.

Five years ago, I had driven past a for sale sign and instantly fell in love with this house. A ranch with three bedrooms, two bathrooms, and a huge backyard. It was an older house from the eighties, but it had been remodeled right before I had moved in. The previous owner had shown me photos before the remodel, and it was mind blowing realizing it was the same house I lived in now. Gone were the wood paneling, dated appliances, and long shag carpet covering the whole house. I wouldn't even go into the ugly wallpaper that had been hung in the bedrooms and bathrooms.

I opened the front door and stepped into the entryway. I dropped my purse on the small bench by the door and held the door open for Playboy.

"Damn, darlin'. You're living the good life."

"Hardly," I muttered. I basically had money for bills and an occasional pizza. That was it. "The kitchen is just through that way." I nodded to the back of the house. "I'm just gonna go change quickly."

Playboy looked me over. "There something wrong with what you have on?"

There wasn't; it was just that they were my work clothes. Blue jeans and a white polo with the Holmes and Gains logo over my heart. "Just want to put something more comfortable on."

Lord, I sounded like one of those girls from the cheesy nineties movies who coyly said they wanted to change into something comfortable when they really meant they wanted to go get all dolled up and sexy. Not what I wanted to do. Should it be, though?

Playboy chuckled and shook his head. "Whatever you want, darlin'."

He headed toward the kitchen, and I ducked down the hallway to my bedroom.

I wasn't changing into something sexy to seduce Playboy. Partly because I didn't have anything that could possibly seduce Playboy. Work polos, t-shirts, jeans, and leggings were the extent of my wardrobe. Even my underwear and bras were boring.

I grabbed the first pair of black leggings in my drawer and pulled on a black Def Leppard sweatshirt. We were totally going for comfy and not impressing Playboy. For all I knew, he was going to eat half of my pizza, tell me he hadn't found anything about Billie Jean, and then leave.

Five minutes later, I stood in front of the bathroom mirror, dragged a brush through my hair, and tossed it into a messy knot on the top of my head.

"Simplicity at its best," I mumbled.

I wandered barefoot back down the hallway and into the kitchen.

Playboy leaned against the kitchen sink, a piece of pizza in one hand, and his phone in the other. He looked down with his thumb on the screen, scrolling.

That was a sight I never thought I would find.

Playboy in my house looked like a real life fantasy. I had seen this porno before.

The hot guy casually in the kitchen, minding his own business when the blonde bombshell walks in and blows his socks off. And his dick.

My cheeks heated, and I knew my B.O.B. was going to be getting a workout tonight after Playboy left. I filed away the thought of blowing Playboy in my kitchen for later.

"Pizza okay?" I called.

Playboy's head snapped up. "That was quick."

"Just needed to change." How long did he think it took to change clothes? Maybe he had thought I was trying to sex myself up for him?

His gaze quickly moved up and down my body. He seemed to do that a lot to me. Was he mentally hoping I looked better or did he like what he saw? He was so hard to read.

"Want a beer?" I asked. I pulled open the fridge and grabbed a bottle of wine. "I also have wine and water."

"Beer is good, pretty girl."

I blinked rapidly at the new endearment. I had been "darlin'" since I met him. Now, I was pretty girl. Not that I really cared about my looks, but it was nice for a guy like Playboy to call me pretty. Though it could be another endearment he used with other women. It sounded different from "darlin'" though. It didn't sound like something he said without even thinking about it.

I grabbed a beer from the bottom shelf and tried to not think about analyzing him calling me "pretty girl." He grabbed the beer from me and twisted off the top. I turned to the counter and set down the bottle of wine. I had no idea what to say to him. I grabbed a wine glass and thought maybe a little liquid courage would help me to start talking more.

"You got plans tonight?" he asked.

I filled my glass to the brim and glanced over my shoulder at him. "Uh, pizza, wine, and TV. Those were my plans for the night." I twisted the cap back on the wine and turned to lean on the counter. Cheap wine in hand and a view full of Playboy. "Why?"

What exactly did he think my plans were for the night? I didn't think I gave off the vibe of being a party girl or anything. This was me during the week.

It was also me on the weekends.

Boring and predictable.

Playboy shrugged. "Just wanted to make sure I wasn't barging in on you when you had other plans."

I shook my head. "This is exactly what I planned on doing."

Playboy took a bite of his pizza. He took a long pull off his beer and set it on the counter next to the pizza. "I haven't found anything about Billie Jean yet. I talked to the guys around the clubhouse but none of them saw or heard anything."

My hopes sank, and I sighed. "That sucks."

"Plan on going to the club tomorrow to see if anyone knows where Billie Jean is."

"I already talked to them," I reminded him. He needed to find Billie Jean, not do the same things I had already tried.

"They might remember something more when I talk to them."

I rolled my eyes. "Really?"

"Got a way with people, pretty girl." He pointed to the patch on his chest. "This right here tends to make people spill their guts with little persuasion."

Well, he might have a point there. A couple of the girls from the club I had talked to before, but most of them had looked at me like I was an outsider they didn't have a spare second for. "We could go tonight to talk to them," I suggested.

We didn't need to wait 'til tomorrow. Each day that went by with no word from Billie Jean, my hope of finding her faded a little bit more.

Playboy shoved the last bite of pizza into his mouth and shook his head. "Monday night. Half the girls aren't even working. Tomorrow, most of them will be back."

I hadn't thought about that. "Oh, well. I guess you're right."

Playboy chuckled and grabbed his beer and the box of pizza. "Lead the way to the TV, pretty girl. I don't want to get in the way of your plans tonight."

"Uh, you're staying?" I really thought he would eat, tell me what he needed, and then leave. It was a surprise that he wanted to stay and watch TV.

"For a little bit, if you don't mind. Jinx was watching some trash TV when I left."

I grabbed the bag of breadsticks and snagged a couple of napkins with my pinky. "Uh, do I want to know what trash TV is?" I laughed. I led the way to the living room and set the breadsticks down on the coffee table.

"Some reality show. He's fucking obsessed with it. *Something Shore*. Horrible fucking accents and people acting like idiots." He set down the pizza and flopped onto the couch. He flipped the lid back on the box and grabbed another slice.

I grabbed a slice and sat down next to him. "Uh, do you mean *Jersey Shore*?"

"Yeah, that's it," Playboy grumbled.

I didn't know if I had seen Jinx, but it was hard to believe any of the guys from the Royal Bastards would watch *Jersey Shore*. "Well, I don't watch *Jersey Shore*, but I don't know if you'll like what I watch any better."

Playboy glanced at me. "Anything is better than that shit."

I took a bite of my pizza and grabbed the remote. "Well, I'm in the middle of watching *Stranger Things*."

"Never heard of it."

I sat back, shocked. "How have you not heard of *Stranger Things*? It's one of the most popular shows on Netflix."

"That an app or something like that?"

I blinked twice and tried to wrap my head around Playboy not knowing what *Stranger Things* was and calling Netflix an app or something. "Do you live under a rock?"

Playboy chuckled and shook his head. "No, pretty girl. I don't live with my head in my phone or my eyes glued to the TV."

I wasn't one to be glued to my phone, but if I was home, the TV was always on. Even if it was for background noise. "So what do you do?"

Playboy threw his head back and laughed. "Ride my bike. Shit with the club. Ride my bike some more."

I tipped my head to the side. "And you never watch TV?"

He shook his head. "I didn't say never, but I'm not addicted to any damn show. Only thing I'm addicted to is the wind at my back and my ass on my Harley."

"You were staring at your phone when I walked into the kitchen."

Playboy pulled out his phone. "I was trying to figure out how to open my fucking voicemail. I've got like fifty million voicemails, and I can't figure out how to listen to them. Figured with you changing, I had some time to figure it out."

I grabbed Playboy's phone and was shocked how old it was. "What is this?" I laughed. It was an old iPhone 5 that had a cracked screen. "You know you can upgrade this, right?"

It's not like I was a slave to technology, but I liked to keep my phone up to date with the latest model. Playboy was about seven years behind on upgrading his phone.

"All I need is for the thing to call and text."

I hit the home button and swiped up. He didn't even have a passcode to unlock it. "You have ninety-nine voicemails."

"That's it?" Playboy asked. "Thought it was a hell of a lot more than that."

"It can only hold that many. I'm sure people have tried to leave more messages, but your voicemail is full." I clicked on the voicemail icon. "I'm assuming you don't know what your password is."

He shook his head. "Negative."

"What's the last four of your phone number?" I asked.

"Uh, seven, four, two, one?" He didn't sound too sure about that.

I typed in the numbers and turned the phone to him. It had worked. "You really want to listen to all of these?"

"You got it?" Playboy, astonished. "I've been trying to do that shit for years. The fucking little envelope picture drove me crazy."

I rolled my eyes. "The last four of your phone number is usually the password they give you and you're supposed to change it." Obviously that didn't happen because Playboy couldn't even get into his voicemail. "You want me to change it for you?"

Playboy shook his head. "Nah. I think I can remember what it is now, and you can delete all of those messages."

"You're sure?" I scrolled through the dates on the messages. The most recent one was from twenty fourteen. It was twenty twenty. Yeah, I was pretty sure whatever the message was didn't matter anymore.

"Delete 'em all," Playboy grunted. "Then turn the fucking voicemail shit off."

I rolled my eyes and did a mass delete of all of his messages. "It's kind of surprising to find someone nowadays who isn't into their phone." I finished up deleting his messages and handed it back to him.

Playboy tossed it on the coffee table. "I'd rather leave the fucking thing at the club, but I need it on me if Barracuda needs me. He and the guys at the club are basically the only ones who have my number."

That was why he hadn't given me his number. He didn't hand it out. I started the next episode of *Stranger Things* and settled into the couch. "Such a basic life," I remarked.

"My life is far from basic, pretty girl." He kicked up his feet on the coffee table.

There was the "pretty girl" again. "Do you know my name?"

He turned his head to look at me. "That a serious question?"

I shrugged. "Just wondering. You don't really call me it."

"It's Raelyn, pretty girl."

Even when he said my name, he still called me "pretty girl." "You call all of the girls that?" The question was out of my mouth before I could stop it.

"Only the ones I like."

I gasped and snapped my mouth shut. *Say what?* He could still call all of the girls that because he liked all of the girls, but it also meant that he liked me. Right? Why did it feel like I was catapulted back to high school and I was trying to figure out if my crush liked me or not?

Except Playboy wasn't a crush.

A man like Playboy wasn't some crush. He was a whole hell of a lot bigger than that.

"Now are you gonna shut up, relax, and watch whatever shit this is?"

The opening credits rolled on the screen, and I nodded. Maybe keeping my mouth shut for an hour would be a good thing. I seemed to be doing a whole hell of a lot more talking than I usually did.

I finished my slice of pizza and grabbed another.

Playboy drained his beer and nodded to my glass that was still full. "Better catch up, pretty girl." He walked back into the kitchen.

I heard him open the fridge. "I didn't know we were having a competition." I grabbed my glass and took a sip.

Playboy walked back into the living room and plopped back down, but this time, he was closer to me. He clicked his beer to my glass. "Bottoms up."

"Is that a toast?" I laughed.

He took a long pull from his beer. "Just a suggestion."

I rolled my eyes and took another sip. "I'm not much of a chugger."

"Figured you weren't."

I wanted to be offended, but I couldn't be. I really wasn't a chugger. "Can we watch the show now?"

He motioned to the TV. "Watch away, pretty girl. Pretend I'm not even here."

That was damn near impossible. Even if he didn't talk, I could just *feel* his presence. Not to mention that he was sitting so close to me that I could now smell his scent. I wasn't sure if it was an actual cologne he wore or if it was just the yummy, manly scent he had. *Keep your mouth shut and do not ask him, Raelyn.*

I kept my mouth shut, but I added it to the ever mounting pile of questions I had for Playboy.

*

Playboy

Was this how I usually spent my Monday nights?

Hell no.

Did I like it, though?

Fuck yes.

The banter flowed between Raelyn and me, and before I knew it, I had drank a six pack and it was half past eleven. We had watched three episodes of this weird ass show, and she had knocked out ten minutes ago.

Her head was resting on the back of the couch, and her face was tipped toward me. Her glasses were crooked, and long lashes brushed her cheeks.

I had heard people talk about natural beauty before, but I had never seen it. At least, not until I had met Raelyn. Her sweet innocence mixed with her fierce need to find her sister made me see her for more than what met the eye. Though what met the eye was fucking stunning.

I didn't need to come over tonight. I could have easily texted her that I hadn't found anything out yet, but I needed to come here to see if what I felt for her was still the same. Had I just been taken by the fact she was different than all of the other girls I had been with? She hadn't thrown herself at me, but she had offered herself to me if I helped find her sister.

There was an attraction between us. I could feel it, and I knew she could, too. The thing that surprised me was she didn't throw herself at me. When she had gone to change her clothes, I thought for sure she was turning into every other girl and was going to walk out in some skimpy shit.

Yeah, that didn't fucking happen. She walked out looking like she was ready for bed…and not bed as in fucking. Bed as in ready to fall the fuck asleep until morning.

I grabbed the remote and turned off the TV.

What the fuck was I doing here?

Raelyn wasn't my type of girl. She deserved shit a hundred times better than I could ever give her. Just look at the fucking house she lived in.

A nice fucking neighborhood, manicured lawns, and a house too good for me to even step foot in. I was a cocky fucker who would never admit that someone was better than me, but a blind man could see I wasn't good enough to talk to Raelyn, let alone sit on her couch and watch her sleep.

But she wanted me here. She invited me in. Shared a meal with me and didn't once act like she wanted me to leave. As long as she wanted me here, I wasn't going to leave. I was a selfish bastard, and I was going to take every second she wanted to give me.

*

Chapter Five

Raelyn

The biker dude...

"You look like you had a good night."

I dropped my purse on my desk. "Uh, I do?" I had walked in the door and headed straight to my work area. I had no idea what Leona was talking about.

"That smile on your face." Leona grabbed her coffee cup from under the coffee maker and set mine under it. She popped in another pod and closed the lid.

I frowned. "What smile?"

Leona laughed. "The one you just wiped off of your face." She pressed the start button and leaned against the counter.

She and I were the only two who worked in the office. Partly because the office wasn't that big. Post and Boomer, our bosses, tended to be on site for all of the jobs and rarely actually came into the office for more than a few minutes to drop off a list of things they needed or something. We had a small area right by the door for the rare walk-ins, a kitchen area to the left of Leona's desk, and then my desk sat on the opposite wall. Post and Boomer had desks, but they were pushed to the back and piled high with samples and what not.

I plopped down in my chair and sighed. I *had* been smiling, and the reason for that smile was Playboy. He had left by the time I woke up this morning, but the text he had sent me on the way to work put the smile on my lips.

7:30. See you tonight.

Yeah, I was going to see him again tonight. I know he had said he was heading to the club tonight to ask around about Billie Jean, so I figured I was going along.

And, I also had his phone number now. The number no one had except for his club buddies.

"Just decided to have a good morning." I turned on my computer and flipped open my schedule book for the day. "And I had Dough's last night. You know how good their pizza is."

Leona grabbed my cup of coffee and splashed some creamer in. "Well, I guess you're right. Good pizza can be the replacement for sex if you're desperate."

"Leona," I laughed. "I wasn't talking about sex."

She set my coffee on my desk and folded her arms over her chest. "Girl, we are both single. The lack of sex is always on our minds."

I grabbed my cup and took a sip. "Speak for yourself."

"Oh, is that so? You have a new man I don't know about or did you get a new toy?" She wagged her finger at me. "You know you better give me the link to buy my own or we're gonna fight."

I rolled my eyes. "No new toy." B.O.B. was doing his job just fine.

"Then I'm gonna need all of the details on the man who seems to be keeping you satisfied."

I set my cup down and typed in my password to get started on my work for the day. Leona and I had the run of the office, but we still had work to do. Though, Leona seemed to always find time in her schedule to chit chat for a while, whether it be with me or her family on the phone.

"There aren't any details." I hadn't told Leona Billie Jean was missing. The more people I told about her being missing, the more real it made it feel. I just needed Playboy to help me find her, and I could stop worrying.

"Raelyn," she whined. "I know something is going on with you."

There was no way she could know anything. "There isn't anything." I did not need to tell her about Playboy. No way, no how.

She leaned forward and splayed her hands on my desk. "I drove by your house last night," she said slowly.

Uh oh.

"I had to turn around and drive by again because I couldn't believe what I saw."

Double uh oh.

"You can only imagine how shocked I was when I saw a motorcycle sitting in front of your house. Luckily, by the time I turned around, there was a god damn man standing on your front porch smoking a cigarette." She turned around and cupped her hands around her mouth. "A man smoking a cigarette," she shouted to the empty office. She whirled back around. "Give. Me. The. Details," she demanded.

"It's nothing," I insisted. At least, it wasn't yet.

"Raelyn, it has been eleven months and thirteen days since a man has looked my way, let alone plundered my woman cave. Even if the guy just stopped to ask for directions, I'm gonna need to know what happened every single time. If it's really juicy, I might have to get my desk toy out and head to the bathroom."

"Leona!" I gasped. "You better not have a B.O.B. in your desk!"

She shrugged and folded her arms over her chest. "I'm not saying I do, but I'm not saying I don't."

"There's something majorly wrong with you," I muttered.

"Yeah," she shouted. "I haven't had a good dicking in almost a year. Now spill the beans about motorcycle dude."

Geesh. I knew Leona hadn't had a boyfriend for a while, but she was obviously going through something if she was ready to pull out her B.O.B. at work. "Dicking?"

"You got five seconds to tell me, Raelyn, or I swear to God, I will explode."

As if she hadn't just exploded? "I can't find Billie Jean and Playboy is helping me find her."

Leona blinked rapidly. "You just said a lot, and I didn't expect any of it." She shook her head and held up a finger. "What do you mean you can't find Billie Jean?"

"I haven't talked to her in a week."

"And why am I now just hearing about it?" she demanded.

"I...well..." I closed my eyes and tried to fight back the sudden urge to cry. "Because I don't know what to do, and I didn't know how to tell you. Her phone is still on, but she's not answering it."

"How do you know it's still on?"

See, I wasn't the only one who didn't know that if it rang it meant it was powered on. Though, I never really had to think about it before. "Because it doesn't go straight to voicemail."

"Oh. I'd like to say that's good news, but I really don't know. Did you go to the police?"

I shook my head. "No. I'm worried they won't care that she's missing because there isn't any evidence that something happened to her. I'm sure once they figure out that her phone was still on, they would write it off as she took off to blow off some steam and will come back when she's ready to."

"Well, shit," Leona mumbled. "I'm sure it won't help any when they ask you what she does for a living and you say work at a strip club."

Nope. That wouldn't help at all. I shook my head sadly. "I didn't know what else to do."

"Is this where the biker dude called Playboy comes into play?"

I nodded. "Billie Jean mentioned him a couple of times and how he helped her out."

"Okay," Leona drawled.

"And, so, I tracked him down and asked if he would help me," I said simply.

"How exactly did you track him down?"

I cleared my throat. "Well, his club owns the strip club, and I knew where the club was…" I trailed off because I could tell Leona was going to freak out at my next words.

"You hauled your cookies to the Royal Bastards' clubhouse and just knocked? Do you understand who the Royal Bastards are?" Leona shrieked.

I knew who they were. Everyone in town knew who they were. "They're a motorcycle club."

Leona flounced over to her desk and grabbed her phone. "Honey, that is putting it pretty fucking plainly." She diddled on her phone and then walked back over to me. She handed her phone to me. "Read that and tell me if they're just a motorcycle club."

I saw the headline and handed it back to her. I had already read that. I had also read the other sixteen articles that mentioned the Royal Bastards before I had gone to the clubhouse. "All of those charges were dropped."

Leona rolled her eyes. "Well, then they must be saints," Leona remarked.

"They aren't." And that was what had convinced me to go to the clubhouse. Whatever had happened to Billie Jean might need the kind of man who would do whatever it took. The law be damned.

"Are you off your rocker, Raelyn?" She reached out and plastered her palm on my forehead. "You feel a little warm."

I knocked her hand away. "I'm feeling fine, Leona. I need to find my sister, and the Royal Bastards are going to help me."

"Why?"

"I just told you why."

She shook her head. "I mean why are they going to help you? Specifically Playboy. It's not like he had a thing going with Billie Jean or anything."

I rolled my eyes. "Because I asked him to help me."

She eyed me closely. "What did you offer them to help you?"

"I don't think that's any of your business, Leona."

"He's getting to dick you in exchange for helping to find your sister."

Jesus. She guessed it right on the first try. "I really need to get my work done for the day."

"Because your biker is coming over tonight?"

I glared at her.

She held up her hands. "Hey, I'm not judging you. I think you're fucking brilliant for striking that deal. Jealous, if I'm telling the truth."

"Leona."

She leaned toward me. "I wanna help you find Billie Jean."

"What?" How in the hell was Leona going to help me? "I have Playboy helping me."

"And now you have me."

I shook my head. "No, Leona. You're not helping me."

"I am and I will. I'll come over tonight, and we can go over everything you know."

"No," I snapped.

She squinted, and a smile spread across her lips. "He *is* coming over tonight."

I clamped my lips shut.

"Girl, you can bet your ass I am coming over tonight to meet biker dude."

"His name is Playboy," I growled.

"Oh, girl. You bet you picked a good one with that name."

"You're not coming over. I won't answer the door."

"I'll be over at seven."

Shit. "No."

"Yes."

"Leona, gosh darn it. You are not going out with Playboy and me tonight," I snapped.

Her eyes lit up. "Oh, baby. You've got a date with biker dude."

Gah. I needed to keep my mouth shut. "No, I don't."

"Where are we going?" She was not going to let this go.

"Nowhere, and it's not a date."

She sat on the edge of my desk. "I'm not giving up, Raelyn. Just spill the beans on what time I need to come to your house and what I should wear."

"He's picking me up at eight thirty, and we're going to Skinz to talk to some people. It's not a date. We're trying to find my missing sister."

Leona clasped her hands together and smiled wide. "Awesome. I'll be at your house at six-thirty because I'm sure you lied about what time he's picking you up."

"Leona," I whined. "Can you please just not come over?" I was beyond desperate for her to stay away. If Leona was at my house when Playboy showed up, I was positive he would turn around before he even got off his bike.

"I wonder what I should wear." She tapped her finger on her chin. "We're asking questions, so maybe something sort of stealthy, yeah?"

"No, Leona." Oh, my God. She was plotting her outfit to wear tonight.

"But, we're doing the questioning at a strip club." She slipped off my desk and wandered back over to hers. "So, a sexy stealthy."

"That's not a thing, Leona, and you are not coming with us tonight."

She smiled over her shoulder. "Oh, yes, I am."

I dropped my chin to my chest and sighed. Dear God. What I had done? I should have just kept my mouth shut. I was horrible at lying or even just stretching the truth.

Should I text Playboy and tell him that Leona was insisting on coming?

Ugh. If I did that then he might not come over at all.

I wasn't going to tell him, and I just prayed that Leona played it cool when Playboy came over tonight.

"Oh, my God," she yelped. "You are not going to believe the cute black skirt I just found online. It's perfect for questioning."

I groaned. Yeah, this was going to be an interesting night.

*

Chapter Six

Playboy

Come again?

"Where are you going?"

I grabbed my cut and shrugged it on. "Gotta pick something up and then to the club."

Mace nodded. "You still looking for Billie Jean?"

"Maybe. Who's asking?"

"Just trying to figure out what you're up to."

I ran my fingers through my hair. "Just helping someone out."

"Since when do you do that?" Mace laughed.

Since a chick like I had never met before asked me to help her. "You make me sound like a dick."

"Brother, you care about one thing in life and it sure in hell isn't helping people."

I flipped him off. "Fuck you."

Mace laughed. "Thanks, but I'll pass. You're not really my type. You looking for that shit, you should hit up Tank."

"Not my speed either, brother." I pulled my keys out of my pocket. "See you at the club later?"

Mace shrugged. "Not sure. I'll see what I feel like later."

I gave him a nod and headed out to my bike.

Mace's words stuck in me like a thorn. The guys had made jokes like that forever, but for some reason, this time, it hit me wrong. I wasn't so selfish of a bastard that I didn't help people.

At least, I didn't think I was.

Maybe the guys saw something that I didn't.

I threw my leg over my bike and started it up. She rumbled underneath me, and I knocked the kickstand up. I roared out of the clubhouse and in the direction of Raelyn's house.

Maybe helping Raelyn was me turning over a new leaf. I needed the motivation to start helping out more and not only giving a shit about myself. Though, the reason I was helping Raelyn was because I wanted her in my bed, so in the end, this all came back to me wanting something for myself.

I guess one couldn't change instantly.

Ten minutes later, I pulled into Raelyn's driveway and saw there were two cars parked.

Raelyn's and another car.

What the fuck was this?

Raelyn's front door opened, and she came jogging down the front steps in bare feet. She was wearing only a black tank top and jeans. "I'm so sorry," she whisper shouted. She skidded to a stop in front of me and laid a hand on my chest when she rocked forward.

"Where are your shoes, pretty girl?" I chuckled.

She dropped her hand from my chest and looked down at her feet.

Eight of her toes were painted gold, and the big toes were painted red. Different.

"Leona was in the bathroom, and I saw you pulled up so I bolted out the door before I could get shoes on."

I reached out and brushed a finger against the skin of her bare arm. "And the rest of your clothes."

Her head snapped up, and she took a step back. "That too."

"He's here!"

What in the fuck?

Raelyn spun around and pointed her finger at a chick hanging out the front door. "You promised."

The woman held up her hands. "I'll just finish getting ready." She stepped back into the house but stood on the other side of the glass screen door.

"You get a roommate?"

Raelyn slowly turned back to face me. "Uh, not exactly." She bit her lip and looked up at me with her icy blue eyes. "Leona works with me and is a level ten stalker."

I tipped my head to the side. "You had me and then lost me."

Raelyn groaned. "Uh, she's worked with me for forever. She knows me better than I know myself. I walked into work with a huge smile on my face, and she sniffed on over to my desk to find out why. I said this; she said that. I told her to shut up; she talked about her office B.O.B., and then I told her no, and now, she's here. Dig me?"

"Clear as mud, pretty girl." Not a fucking clue what she was talking about.

Raelyn dropped her chin to her chest. "She's coming with us." She tipped her head back. "I. Am. Sorry."

I looked back at the door. Her friend was still standing there. "And why is she coming with us?" I hadn't even told Raelyn where we were going.

"Because I told her about Billie Jean, and then you. Then she ranted about well…things, and now she's coming."

"Things?" I asked.

Her cheeks turned pink. "Uh, things that really don't need to be repeated."

"And who is Bob?" I had no clue where Raelyn worked and had a sliver of jealousy creep in at the name of Bob.

She shook her head. "Also something that doesn't need to be repeated." She pointed to her car. "I can drive us."

I looked at her car. There was nothing wrong with it other than it was a car. I didn't ride in cages often. "We're taking my bike."

She tipped her head to the side and looked toward my bike. "Uh, you really think all three of us are going to fit on there."

I pulled my phone out. "No. You're the only one who's going to ride with me. Go finish getting dressed."

"Are we ditching Leona?" she asked hopefully.

I shook my head. I fucking wished we could, but I figured just bringing her along would be easier. "She can ride with Mace."

Mace had said he didn't know if he was going to the club, but I had just made up his mind for him.

"Oh," Raelyn mumbled. "Is he okay with that?"

"Leave that to me to worry about." I nodded to the house. "Get dressed, pretty girl. Fifteen minutes."

"Uh, okay." She sprinted back to the front door. "You're sure you're okay with this?" she called when she was halfway.

I wasn't entirely okay with it, but it wasn't that big of a deal. If anything, it would give Mace a little entertainment for the night and I would have Raelyn to myself. "It's fine," I reassured her.

She raised her hand in the air and slipped back into the house.

I connected the call to Mace and leaned against Raelyn's car.

"What's up, ballbag?" Mace called into the phone.

"Need some help."

"What the hell do you need help with?" he chuckled. "You said you were picking something up and heading to the club."

"Yeah," I sighed. "Turns out, I'm picking up two things and I don't have room for both."

"What in the fuck are you doing?"

"Just fucking get here." I rattled off Raelyn's address and ended the call.

This was what I got for actually helping someone. I pulled out a cigarette and shoved it in my mouth. I had been half thinking if things went well at the club with Raelyn tonight, we could head back to her house and start working on the other part of our agreement. With her friend tagging along, and now Mace coming, things weren't going the way I planned at all.

Ten minutes later, after I smoked three cigarettes, I heard loud pipes in the distance. About thirty seconds later, Mace pulled into the driveway.

He parked next to my bike and shut it off. "What in the fuck are you doing in this part of town?" he hollered.

I rolled my eyes and dropped my cigarette on the driveway. I ground it out with my toe and moved toward Mace. "You think you could keep your fucking voice down?" I was sure Raelyn's neighbors were already wondering what the hell was going on over here with my bike being parked on the street most of last night.

"Bro, do you see where we're parked? Unless this is your fucking grandma's house, I don't know what the hell you think you're picking up here."

"Oh, my God. They're multiplying."

Mace looked over my shoulder and pulled his sunglasses off his face. "Well, shit," he mumbled.

I turned to the sound of Raelyn's friend. She was talking, but I was looking at Raelyn.

She looked nothing like she had ten minutes ago.

Her silky hair was down in waves around her shoulders; her lips were painted a light pink, and her eyes had a dusting of peach on them which was only enhanced by the dark frames of her glasses.

She was wearing the same jeans she had been before, but now, she had on a black shirt that hung off one shoulder over the tank top. Her bare feet were gone and covered with black heeled boots. She was dressed simple, but she was without a doubt the most beautiful woman I had ever laid eyes on.

Her friend was definitely a looker, but she was nothing compared to Raelyn.

"This what you needed help picking up?" Mace asked.

I glanced over my shoulder and nodded.

"Do I get to call dibs on one?"

I curtly shook my head. "You get the blonde."

Mace shrugged. "Not my first choice, but I'm willing to adapt. Surprised to see your tastes have changed, though."

Raelyn's friend was my typical type, but she wasn't doing anything for me. Raelyn was the only chick I wanted right now.

"Uh, everything okay?" Raelyn called.

"How is everything not okay with these two handsome men in our presence?" Her friend extended her hand to me. "I'm Leona. Raelyn was kind enough to invite me along for our little excursion tonight."

"Invite?" Raelyn scoffed. "Pretty sure I told you no four times, if not more."

Leona flitted her hand at Raelyn. "Details, babe."

I hitched my thumb over my shoulder toward Mace. "That's Mace. He's your ride for the night, Leona."

Leona batted her eyes at Mace. "Charmed to meet you." She strutted over to him and laid her hand on his shoulder as she threw her leg over the bike.

"Are you sure this is okay?" Raelyn asked me softly. "If you don't want both of us coming with you, we can just stay home."

"We're good, pretty girl." We were. Not exactly what I wanted for tonight, but it was going to be fine. Mace obviously knew I was interested in Raelyn and would keep Leona busy the whole night. "Let's go."

She followed me over to my bike and waited while I climbed on. "Been on a bike before?" I asked.

She nodded. "I used to drive a dirt bike in high school."

"Dirt bike?" I asked, amazed. I did not expect her to say that. I figured she hadn't ever been on a bike before.

"Yeah. It was the only thing I could afford." She got on behind me without hesitation and rested her arms around my waist.

"You lock up?"

"Yup."

I cranked up the bike and backed around.

"Club?" Mace called over the roar of our engines.

"Yeah," I called.

I headed in the direction of the club with Raelyn at my back and Mace following behind with Leona.

Time to figure out where the fuck Billie Jean was.

*

Chapter Seven

Raelyn

Try to keep your mouth shut…

I had been on a bike before, but it had been almost eight years. As soon as I had graduated from high school, I had traded in my dirt bike and gotten an actual car. In that time, I had forgotten how freeing it was to be on a motorcycle. Add in the fact I was wrapped around Playboy and it was even better.

Fifteen minutes later, we pulled into the parking lot of Skinz and parked in the front row

"Perks of owning the place?" I asked when Playboy turned off the bike.

"Definitely, pretty girl."

"Looks like 'cuda and Monk are here," Mace called.

"Who is 'cuda?" Raelyn asked.

"Prez and Monk is our VP," I answered.

I slid off the bike and stood off to the side. "Is it bad that they're here?" she asked.

Playboy shook his head. "Nah. Pretty typical for most of the club to be here. 'cuda and Monk tend to move in tandem, though."

Yeah, no idea what that meant. "They don't know anything about Billie Jean?"

Playboy shook his head and got off the bike. "Haven't heard anything."

That sucked.

Mace and Leona had parked next to us, and it looked like they had snuggled up pretty closely. Maybe Leona was going to end her drought of a love life tonight.

Playboy grabbed my hand. "Stay with me in the club, yeah?"

I tried to focus on his words and not the feel of his hand wrapped around mine. I tipped my head back and nodded. "Okay."

"I mean it, Raelyn. You gotta go to the bathroom, you tell me and I'll take you, okay."

That seemed a bit drastic, but this was Playboy's world. I was just living in it until I figured out where Billie Jean had disappeared to. "Got it. You and I are stuck together like glue." Gah. Here I thought maybe I had stopped saying stupid things in front of Playboy.

Yeah. Not so much.

"I can pee alone, yeah?" Leona asked.

Mace slid his sunglasses on top of his head. "Do whatever you want, doll."

Playboy led us into the club, and I trailed behind him with my hand in his. Walking into the club this time was way different than the last time.

I didn't have to stand in line. I didn't have to show them my ID.

Everyone seemed to stare at us, though. I scooted closer to Playboy as we wove through the crowd and tables. He glanced over his shoulder at me and gave a nod. "Stay close."

I could totally do that.

Hell, I *liked* that.

"Drinks," Mace called. He split off from us with Leona in tow.

I had the urge to grab her hand and keep her with me, but she seemed to be more in her element than I was. Leona was definitely more outgoing and fit in here.

She had tried to make me dress up a bit, and while I didn't wear my typical sweatshirt, I still looked pretty much like I always did.

Leona, on the other hand, had black, skintight pants encasing her ass, a red cropped top with bell sleeves over her ample chest, and silver booties on her feet. Her blond hair was piled on top of her head, and it didn't look like the wind on the ride over had messed it up at all.

I knew for a fact that my curled hair looked like a rat's nest on my head. This was why no one ever looked my way. The art of looking good was completely lost on me.

Playboy led us to the other side of the club to a cluster of roped off tables where only a couple of guys were seated.

They were both wearing cuts, and I assumed they were Barracuda and Monk.

Meeting the president of the Royal Bastards was *not* what I thought we would be doing tonight. Playboy pulled out one of the chairs at the table and motioned for me to sit down.

Yeah, sitting with the president of an MC was something I did *all* of the time. I nervously sat down, and Playboy dropped into the chair next to me.

Both men stared at me.

I sat there frozen like a deer caught in the headlights of a huge semi barreling down on it.

I lifted my hand and gave a wave.

Yeah, I waved.

If God didn't strike me down right then and there from embarrassment then there wasn't a God.

Playboy chuckled and rested his arm around my shoulders. He leaned close, and his lips brushed my ear. "Relax, pretty girl. They don't bite."

Easier said than done. And, it looked like both of them bit. Hard.

"New blood?" the guy to the left asked.

"Billie Jean's sister, Monk." Playboy replied.

That helped. Now I at least knew who was who.

"Is she still missing?" the one who must have been Barracuda asked.

I nodded. "I haven't heard from her for a week." I didn't know if I was supposed to speak, but I did.

"You sure she didn't take a breather for a minute?" Monk asked.

I nodded again. "Yeah. Billie Jean wouldn't leave town without giving me a heads up. I talked to her before she came to work, and then, I didn't hear from her again."

Playboy relaxed next to me and kept his arm around me. "Figured I'd talk to the girls tonight and see if I can find anything out."

Barracuda nodded. "Good place to start." There was an arrogant air about Barracuda. His words were simple enough, but he seemed to be giving Playboy permission to talk to the girls.

Leona sat down next to me with a drink in her hand. "Did you see the shoes the waitress with the red hair was wearing?"

"Uh," I mumbled. I hadn't really looked at anything as Playboy and I walked through the club. I had been in shock at the fact that he was holding my hand. "I'll have to keep an eye out for her."

Leona nodded. "Girl, they are hot." She smiled wide. "Not that I expected a waitress at a strip club to wear Crocs or something."

"Doll, you think you could have grabbed one of these drinks?" Mace grumbled. He set a drink in front of me and sloshed some of it on the table. He sat next to Playboy and did not seem amused with Leona.

Leona leaned toward me and lowered her voice. "I pissed him off," she whispered. "I wasn't paying attention to him walking in front of me and barreled right into him when he stopped at the bar."

"What were you looking at?" I hissed back.

Leona cringed. "The redhead's shoes."

"You're a mess, Leona," I laughed. "I'm the one supposed to be making a fool of themselves, not you."

"Well, I guess it's finally my turn."

I took a sip of my drink. "Well, I gave a princess wave to the president and VP of the Royal Bastards. Maybe we're both destined to make fools of ourselves tonight."

Leona cringed. "Is that who those two are?"

I nodded.

"I'm gonna try to keep my mouth shut. Maybe we both should."

That sounded like a damn good idea. I just hoped that both of us could stick to it.

"Billie Jean was close with Raine and Violet. Start there," Barracuda instructed.

Playboy nodded.

Was it just Playboy helping me, or was the whole club helping me? "Uh, I talked to Raine last week but not Violet. Raine said she didn't know anything about Billie Jean. She figured she was home sick or something when she didn't show up for her shifts."

"But she showed up Tuesday night, right?" Playboy asked.

I nodded. "She worked last Tuesday with Billie Jean. She said Billie Jean was her normal self."

"Sassy and full of it?" Mace laughed.

That was pretty accurate. "Yeah. That's Billie Jean to a T."

"This a class field trip or something?" Monk asked. He looked from Leona to me.

Playboy might be fine with Leona tagging along to help figure out where Billie

Jean was, but Monk obviously didn't think it was necessary.

"How many people know Billie Jean is missing?" Barracuda asked.

"Uh, well." I counted the people who knew in my head. It was a short list. "Playboy and Leona are the only ones I told."

"And the people you talked to last week at the club," Playboy pointed out.

"Well, I didn't exactly tell them she was missing, though. I just asked if they had seen her." I guess even asking if they had seen her was hinting to the fact she was missing.

"There's buzz she's missing. Mitzy was telling me earlier the girls were kind of paranoid wondering if something was going on." Barracuda shrugged. "As of right now, I told her nothing was going on and to treat everything like business as usual."

"Mitzy?" Leona muttered to me.

I shrugged. "No clue."

"You think that's his old lady?"

"Ol'," I hissed. "Old lady is like your grandma."

Playboy's eyes cut to me.

I plastered a smile on my lips. "Shut. Up," I grunted to Leona. What happened to keeping her mouth shut? I didn't care if Mitzy was Barracuda's ol' lady. If she had any info about Billie Jean, I wanted to talk to her. "Maybe we should talk to Mitzy, too."

"Have Playboy do the talking," Monk instructed. "The girls know to keep their mouths shut if they're talking to someone they don't know."

"Oh." Well, what was the point of me being here then?

A woman dressed in black tight pants and a skimpy white tank top walked up to our table and leaned toward Barracuda. Their voices were low, and I couldn't make out a word they said.

Leona leaned toward them. "I used to be able to read lips," she muttered.

Dear God. Did she not know how to be less obvious? "Stop it," I hissed.

"There's a bear at the bar, and he left his lettuce in the safe."

Playboy choked on his beer, and I slapped my hand over my face.

"His lettuce in the safe?" Mace asked.

Leona closed one eye and tipped her head to the side. "Pineapple?"

Playboy wiped his mouth with the back of his hand. "Pineapple and lettuce don't even sound the same."

Mace shook his head. "And why is it in his safe?"

The woman walked away, and Barracuda sat back in his chair. "You four done acting like fools?"

Apparently, we weren't talking as quietly as I had thought.

"What did Mitzy want?" Monk asked.

So that was Mitzy. I couldn't get a feel of whether or not they were together.

Barracuda grabbed his drink. "Memphis hasn't shown up for her last four shifts."

Say what?

"Anyone check on her?" Playboy asked.

Barracuda shook his head. "Mitzy said she went to her house before she came in today and she didn't answer the door. Her car was in the parking lot."

"I'll head over there." Monk drained his glass and set it on the table. "Maybe she's just passed out inside or something."

I looked at Playboy.

He shook his head and leaned close. "Just stay calm, pretty girl. This might have nothing to do with Billie Jean."

It was too much of a coincidence, though. Billie Jean was missing, and now, another girl from the club was gone.

Barracuda stared at me. "Stop by Billie Jean's on your way back, Monk," he called.

Even Barracuda knew something was going on.

I cringed and felt deflated. "Uh, I didn't bring the key to her apartment with me."

Monk smirked and stood. "I think I'll make do without it." He walked away from the table and into the crowd of people.

"I'm assuming he doesn't need her address either," I mumbled.

"Talk to the girls. See what you can find out about Memphis and Billie Jean," Barracuda instructed Playboy and Mace. He turned to Leona and me. "You two stay here."

"What?" Leona scoffed. "How are we supposed to help find Billie Jean and now Memphis if we just sit here?"

Barracuda leaned back in his chair and folded his arms over his chest. "Because from the looks of you two, you've never stepped foot in a strip club before and it's best if you kept your asses planted in those seats."

"Billie Jean is my sister," I pointed out. "No one here would even be looking for her if it wasn't for me. I need to be the one out there looking for her."

Playboy laid his hand on my arm. "Just stay here, pretty girl. Mace and I will split up and be back quick."

"That's not fair," Leona pouted. "I was all ready to get my Nancy Drew on tonight." She held up her purse. "You would be surprised at the things I managed to cram into here."

Barracuda nodded to Playboy and Mace. "Go. I'll keep an eye on these two."

Mace gladly stood and took off toward the stage where a woman was swinging around on a pole. Playboy pressed a kiss to the side of my head and walked in the opposite direction of Mace.

I watched him disappear into the crowd and tried not to squeal at the fact he had kissed me. Granted, it was the side of my head, but it was still a kiss.

My feelings were like on a huge pendulum that swung back and forth. First, I was sad about Billie Jean being missing, but then, Playboy would send me a text or kiss the side of my head and I was carefree and giddy about Playboy. I was going to get whiplash from bouncing around all of the time.

Leona sighed and set her purse on the table. "I can't believe I'm not going to be able to use my stun gun tonight."

"Stun gun?" Barracuda narrowed his eyes on Leona. "What the hell did you think you would need a stun gun for?"

She shrugged and unzipped the zipper. "One never knows when the occasion might arise where a good stunning is called for."

"Don't you dare empty that thing on this table," Barracuda rumbled.

Leona's fingers froze on the zipper pull. "Uh, what happens if I do?" She batted her eyes at Barracuda.

Oh, Jesus. Now she was going to try to turn her charm on Barracuda. I kicked her under the table and glared at her. "Knock it off," I hissed. Keeping Leona reined in was freaking exhausting.

"I'd kick your ass out and send you home in a taxi." Barracuda tipped his head to the side. "And that's just to start."

"I feel you might have some issues that you're masking with rage and assholiness."

Leona was going to get us kicked out. She had completely forgotten our plan of keeping our mouths shut and had let her crazy ass run free.

Barracuda glared at Leona.

She rested her elbows on the table and plopped her head in her hands. "So, how does one become a president of a badass MC?" she asked. "Is that like a two or four-year degree?"

Yup, Leona was going to get us kicked out of here.

I downed my drink and looked around for the waitress. I was going to need about ten more of these.

*

Chapter Eight

Playboy

Wanna come in?

"She left with a guy."

"A guy?" I asked. Why in the hell would Billie Jean be leaving with a guy after her shift?

Violet nodded and snapped the gum in her mouth. "Yeah."

"You know who the guy was?"

She shook her head. "Never saw him before that night. He sat in her section all night and seemed fine."

"He hit on her or anything?"

Violet rolled her eyes. "Watching Billie Jean isn't really something I can do while I'm waiting on my section." Violet was a straight up bitch. She had tried hitting on me when I first started talking to her, but as soon as she figured out I wasn't interested, she flipped her bitch switch and kept snapping her gum.

I was two seconds away from ripping it from her mouth and shoving it up her ass. "Do you remember what kind of vehicle she was in?"

Violet rolled her eyes. "It was a black car."

"You remember what kind of car?" A black car was pretty fucking vague and made it hard to pinpoint the right one.

"I don't know, Playboy. It was a week ago, and I've got other things on my mind than what kind of car Billie Jean drove off in." She looked over her shoulder to the back door. "Are we done now or do you want to keep eating up my break?"

I turned away from her and headed back to the table where I had left Raelyn. Violet didn't deserve another word from me. Thank Christ I had never given her the time of day.

Barracuda had four beer bottles in front of him and was staring at Leona as she talked with her hands flailing all over.

Raelyn wasn't at the table.

What the fuck?

"Where did Raelyn go?" I demanded when I got to the table.

Leona tipped her head back and tried to focus her glazed over eyes on me. "Howdy there, biker dude." I think she tried to wink at me but just closed her eyes for five seconds and then opened them. I had only been gone for forty-five minutes. Leona was a lightweight, or they were mixing the drinks pretty strong for a Tuesday night.

"She went to the bathroom," Barracuda butted in. "She said she was gonna wait until you came back but couldn't hold it any longer."

"You couldn't go with her?" I asked him.

Barracuda turned his glare on me. "Didn't know I needed to hold your girlfriend's purse while she pissed."

I headed to the bathroom. It wasn't worth it to say anything more to Barracuda. Raelyn wasn't his responsibility so he didn't care about her.

I barged into the women's bathroom and startled Raelyn who was standing in front of the sink washing her hands.

"Playboy," she gasped. She gripped the sink with one hand and held her other to her heart. "What are you doing in here?"

"You weren't at the table."

She blinked quickly. "I was gonna wait until you got back to go to the bathroom but uh, well…"

I had barged in here like a maniac as if she were robbing the place or something. "You could have texted me."

"On your prehistoric phone? I didn't know if you had a text limit or something." She laughed lightly and turned back to the sink.

I moved over to the other sink and leaned against it. "You don't seem to be as wasted as Leona."

"Uh, no. Leona seems to be downing her drinks a little bit faster than I am. She's on number five while I've only just touched number three." She grabbed a paper towel and dried her hands. "The drinks are pretty strong here."

"Not normally. It may have to do with the fact you're sitting with Barracuda and they know not to skimp on the booze when a Royal Bastard is at the table."

She tossed the paper towel in the garbage. "Well, I'll have to remember that if this happens again." She sighed and smiled wonkily. "Getting drunk in a strip club isn't what I normally do on a Tuesday. Or any day, for that matter." She stepped toward me and stumbled.

I grabbed her around the waist and steadied her. "Whoa there, pretty girl."

"I might be a little more tipsy than I thought I was."

"Just a little," I chuckled.

She laid her hands on my chest and tipped her head back to look at me. "This has been the strangest week of my life, and it just keeps getting stranger."

I brushed her hair from her face. "But it's a good strange, right?"

"Parts of it are pretty good," she whispered.

I pulled her close and delved my fingers in her hair. "Time for a good part, pretty girl." My lips brushed against hers, and a sigh escaped her mouth.

She tipped her head back more and leaned into the kiss. Her lips were like velvet, and her taste was as sweet as sugar.

Addictive.

I wanted more but was afraid I would never get enough.

Her hands balled into fists and clenched my shirt.

"More," she gasped when we finally came up for air.

"Later, pretty girl. I don't want the first time I fuck you to be in the women's bathroom at a strip club."

"I'm okay with that." Her eyes bugged out as soon as the words fell from her lips. "I mean…"

I grabbed her hand and pulled her toward the door. "I kind of like it when you blurt out whatever you're feeling without thinking about it."

"Stupid seems to come out of my mouth when you're around," she muttered.

I glanced over my shoulder at her. "Honesty comes out of your mouth, pretty girl."

We walked out of the bathroom, and I sat back down at the table, but this time, I pulled Raelyn onto my lap. I needed to talk to Barracuda about what Violet had told me, but that didn't mean I couldn't have Raelyn close.

Never in my life had I been possessive of a woman before. If one wanted to leave or didn't want me, I would just find another.

With Raelyn around, there wasn't anyone else who could hold my attention. She was more than satisfying everything I wanted and all I had done was kiss her.

Leona pointed her finger at us. "This. This I like," she slurred. "Though I would like it better if it was happening to me, but choosers can't be beggars." She hiccupped loudly and held up her empty cup. "I'm fill. Empty me."

"Oh, Leona," Raelyn laughed. "I think we should probably cut you off. You're going to fall off the back of Mace's bike."

"She's getting a taxi," Mace grumbled.

Somehow Leona and Mace had not hit it off like I had thought they would.

"I'll take her home." Barracuda finished his beer and dropped a fifty on the table.

Oh. Now this was something I didn't see coming.

Leona held her hand out to him. "You've got a deal, Snake."

"Snake?" I asked.

Raelyn laughed. "Leona thinks a barracuda is a snake."

"Well, at first she thought it was a big black cat," Barracuda laughed. "We cleared that one up pretty quickly, though."

"Uh, isn't a large black cat a black panther?" Mace asked. "How the heck do you think a black panther is a barracuda. It's a deadly fish."

Leona sloppily waved her hand at Mace. "Those are all details."

This was going downhill fast. "How about I tell you what I found out and then we can all head out?"

Barracuda nodded. "I haven't heard from Monk yet, but I'm assuming he ain't finding shit."

"Well," I drawled. "I managed to talk to Violet, and she saw Billie Jean drive off in a black car with a guy after her shift Tuesday."

"Oh, my God!" Raelyn gasped. "Who was the guy?"

I shrugged. "Violet said she hadn't seen him before. He hung out in her section for a good part of the night and then she left with him."

"Buuuuut," Leona drawled and interrupted, "Billie Jean likes kitties."

Mace, Barracuda, and I looked at each other trying to figure out what the hell Leona was talking about.

Raelyn drug her hand down her face. "She likes girls, she means. She was saying kitty as like…" Raelyn dropped her eyes. "Down there."

"Pussy?" Mace asked.

Leona tapped her finger to her nose. "Ding, ding. Tell him what he's won, Alex."

"Jesus," Barracuda groaned. I wondered if he was thinking of changing his mind about taking Leona home. "I'll have someone going over the tapes from last Tuesday and see if they can pick anything up. At least it happened on a Tuesday so it won't be as packed. We should be able to pick out guys who aren't regulars."

"But why would she leave with a guy she didn't know?" Raelyn asked.

"Maybe she did know him," Mace suggested. "It sounds like you were close with your sister, but maybe she didn't tell you everything."

Mace's words were harsh, but they hit the truth.

I squeezed her leg. "We'll figure it out, Raelyn."

She looked at me warily. "She wouldn't have gone off with some random guy."

Right now, we didn't know that. Maybe he had tricked her somehow or something.

Barracuda stood up. "I'll have Rebel and Tank go over the video tomorrow. They are here the most so they should be able to pinpoint the guy Violet is talking about."

"Are you still riding me?" Leona shook her head. "I mean am I still riding you?" Leona slowly turned to look at Raelyn. "Am I talking out loud? Tell me I'm dreaming."

Raelyn reached out and patted her hand. "This will all be a faint memory when you wake up in the morning, honey."

"That'll be nice," Leona sighed. "Bye, bye Raelyn and biker dude."

Barracuda managed to get her out of her seat and led her to the exit by only half carrying her.

"You really think she is going to remember any of this?" I asked.

Raelyn shrugged. "For her sake, I hope she doesn't because I'm pretty sure she is going to die of embarrassment if she remembers asking Barracuda if he was going to ride her."

"If she doesn't remember, I'll be sure to remind her the next time I see her," Mace laughed.

"Let's get you home, pretty girl."

*

Raelyn

It was going on nine thirty, and I did have to work in the morning.

We said bye to Mace and headed to the door. Playboy's hand was splayed on my back, and he guided me through the crowd and tables. I watched the woman on stage for a couple of seconds and had to appreciate how easy she made sliding and flipping all over the floor and pole look. If I tried that, I would have ended up on my ass and panting like I had run fifty miles.

"You sure you're okay to ride?" Playboy asked once we were out of the club.

"Yeah. All I have to do is hold and try to lean into the turns." Easy peasy. I looked around to see if Leona was still here, but they must have taken off pretty quickly.

"What's wrong,?" Playboy asked.

"Uh, I was just wondering if Leona was okay. I hope she holds onto Barracuda."

Playboy climbed on the bike, and I got on behind him. I had a slight check of my balance and feared I was going to tip over when I lifted my leg, but I managed to mount the bike without biting the dust.

"She'll be fine, pretty girl, but if you are worried about her, we can give Barracuda a call when we get home."

That was nice of Playboy to offer. I didn't intend to sound as if I was doubting the fact Barracuda would take care of her. He definitely was arrogant, but along with the arrogance, he seemed completely competent.

The drive back to my house was entirely too short, and I had been half tempted to ask Playboy to take the long way home.

We pulled into my driveway fifteen minutes later and parked behind Leona's car.

Playboy followed me to the front door, and I quickly unlocked it. I wasn't sure if he intended to come inside or if he was just walking me in.

I got my answer when I turned around to invite him in and he pulled me into his arms. His lips were on mine and his hands roamed over my back. I grabbed onto his shoulders and just enjoyed the kiss.

I was panting heavily when we finally came up for air. "Wow."

Playboy brushed my hair from my face. "Yeah, kissing you is wow, pretty girl."

Well, that was good to hear. I would hate for me to be enjoying Playboy kissing me and he actually hated it.

"Uh, did you want to come in?" My tone was breathy, and I took a deep gulp of air.

"You got work in the morning?" he asked.

"Uh, well, yeah." That didn't mean he couldn't come in for a little bit. Hell, he could come in for a long bit just as long as he came in.

"Raincheck, pretty girl. I don't want to keep you up two nights in a row."

My hopes sank. I kind of liked him keeping me awake for two nights in a row. Tonight, I was hoping he would keep me awake doing something other than watching a movie. "Oh, okay." I tried to hide my disappointment.

I didn't do too well.

Playboy wrapped me up in his arms and pulled me against him. I buried my face in his chest and inhaled deep.

"You make it mighty hard to leave, Raelyn."

Good. He made it mighty hard for me to not want to be around him. My attraction and dependency to a man I knew only days was slightly scary. If I was already feeling that I didn't want him to leave now, I could only imagine what a few weeks of knowing each other was going to be like. "Then don't leave," I whispered.

He squeezed me tight and sighed. "I'll touch base with you tomorrow, okay?"

Huh. That didn't sound promising at all for him to stay. "Or you could just stay the night and then you could just touch base with me when we wake up."

"So fucking tempting." He pressed a kiss to the side of my head and stepped back. He dropped his arms, and I instantly felt cold.

How? How in the hell was he doing this to me? He said it was hard for him to leave, but it didn't really seem that he was struggling with it that much.

"Sleep sweet, pretty girl." He gave me one last longing look and then turned down the path back to his bike.

I watched his retreating form and held back the urge to run to him or call out his name. I had told him to stay. He knew I was catching feelings for him.

Maybe that was why he was going.

He wanted to stay the night but he didn't want my feelings that went along with him staying.

The more Playboy was around, the more I was getting attached to him.

I could tell he had heartache written all over him, but I couldn't seem to run away from him. I couldn't step back and act like I wasn't feeling anything.

His bike roared to life, but I didn't move. I didn't go into the house.

I watched his headlight bounce across my car and then turn as he backed his bike up.

I clenched my fists and gritted my teeth. Never had I wanted something more in my life.

Playboy revved his engine, and then, he rocketed out of my driveway.

His words echoed in my head as I opened the door and dropped my purse on the floor. There was no way I was going to sleep sweet if Playboy wasn't with me.

*

Chapter Nine

Playboy

Body snatchers…

We forgot to call Barracuda about Leona.

I had been hoping I could try to clear my head, but Raelyn's message was there when I pulled my phone out after I got back to the clubhouse.

Barracuda sat at the bar with a drink in his hand and a frozen pizza in front of him.

"You might want to cook that," I advised.

He flipped me off. "I was working on it." He grabbed his pocketknife and sliced the plastic off.

"Leona get home okay?"

Barracuda shrugged. "I'll let you know."

"Uh, what?" I asked.

Barracuda grabbed the frozen pizza and moved around to the other side of the bar. "She was rambling on about having pizza." He opened the pizza oven and slid the pizza in.

"So, you brought her back here for pizza?"

Barracuda nodded. "Yeah."

I wasn't normally one to question Barracuda seeing as he was the prez, but it seemed a little out of the norm for him to not only give Leona a ride home, but to detour to the clubhouse seemed crazy. "Are you feeling okay?"

He slammed the pizza oven shut and grabbed his drink. "Never better."

I sat at the bar and set down my phone. "Raelyn asked me to check to make sure Leona made it home."

Barracuda sipped his drink. "And?"

"And what the hell am I supposed to tell her?"

He shrugged. "Whatever the fuck you want to, brother. I'm not worried about Raelyn. That's your deal."

That didn't help me whatsoever. **All good. Barracuda took care of her.** Not exactly a lie. He was taking care of her, it just wasn't at her house.

Okay. Thanks. I had fun tonight. Getting tipsy at a strip club was fun? Maybe Raelyn fit into the club scene better than I thought.

Me too, pretty girl.

"You wanna tell me what the hell is going on with her or is that none of my business?"

I shrugged. "Not much to tell."

"See, that's where I think you are wrong. I think there is a whole hell of a lot going on seeing as I haven't seen you in this club with a chick since last Friday."

"Raelyn was here Saturday," I pointed out.

"You know what the fuck I'm talking about," Barracuda growled. "Are you getting hooked on this chick?"

Was I? It sure as hell felt like it, but it was too fucking early to know anything. I wanted to stay with her tonight. Hell, I wanted to fuck her 'til the sun came up and sleep all day with her. That was what I really fucking wanted to do.

But here I was sitting at the clubhouse talking with Barracuda.

"Hard to say."

"What are you, a fucking Magic Eight Ball? Are you bedding the chick or not?"

Barracuda seemed pretty interested in where my dick was. "Bedding her? No. Spending time with her and helping her find her sister? Yeah. That's what I'm doing."

"Fucking body snatchers up in this bitch then. You're staying with one chick and I'm nursing a drunk girl in my room." Barracuda grabbed a bottle of whiskey and filled his glass to the brim.

"From the lack of soda in your drink, it looks like you're trying to figure shit out, too."

He shook his head. "You don't even know half of it, brother."

"Club shit or women shit?"

Barracuda shook his head. "Just shit." He took a long drink from his glass and winced at the burn going down his throat. "I finish this and I won't be thinking about it anymore."

I grabbed my phone and shoved it in my pocket. "Well, you know where to find me if you want to talk."

Barracuda nodded, and I headed to my room.

I wasn't one to be in my room before ten thirty unless it was to do some fucking, but ever since I met Raelyn, I was in my room before midnight and alone.

I'd known the chick for three days, and I was already becoming pussy whipped.

I laughed, and the sound echoed in my room. The hell of it was…I wasn't even getting any pussy.

*

Ten

Raelyn

Slightly stalker-ish…

"I'm not gonna be in today."

I filled my coffee cup and tried not to laugh. "Not feeling good?" I asked into the phone.

Leona groaned. "You know damn well why the hell I'm not coming in. I don't even know what I was drinking last night, but I know I will never ever drink it again."

A low voice rumbled in the background. My jaw dropped, and I gripped the handle of my coffee cup so I didn't drop it. "Who is that?" I demanded.

"Oh, uh. I gotta go." The line went dead, and I stood there staring at the coffee maker and realized Leona had spent the night with Barracuda. Well, at least, I figured it had been Barracuda. No way in hell she would have been able to find another guy after Barracuda dropped her off.

Playboy had texted me last night that Barracuda had taken care of Leona, but I guess I didn't read between the lines.

Hell. I had asked Playboy to spend the night and he hadn't.

Leona got real tipsy and wound up in bed with Barracuda. I guess her dry spell was over.

My phone rang, and Playboy's name flashed across the screen.

"Hello?"

"Hello, pretty girl."

I would never get tired of Playboy calling me that. Never. "I didn't expect to hear from you this early." I carried my coffee cup over to my desk and sat down. With Leona not coming in today, I had more work to do, but I had a couple of minutes I could spare to talk to Playboy.

"Perks of going to bed before midnight. I'm up before the fucking sun."

I laughed and powered on my computer. "Careful. You don't want to ruin your reputation. Nobody cool is ever up before the sun."

"You got jokes and sass this morning, pretty girl."

I watched the progress bar on my computer fill with color. "Perks of being awake before the sun," I parroted.

"Got plans for lunch?"

Hmm. This was totally unexpected. Once I had gotten in the house last night and changed into my pajamas, I had convinced myself that Playboy wasn't interested in me after all and he only kissed me last night because he felt sorry for me. In the daylight, perhaps that wasn't true. "Well, seeing as my co-worker drank herself silly last night and won't be in today, I gotta stay in the office so I'll order something."

"Stay in the office but don't order anything. I'll be over in your area around lunch."

My computer screen flashed, and the home screen appeared. I needed to focus on something other than the fact that Playboy was coming over for lunch. "You know where I work?"

"Yeah."

Hmm. I shouldn't be surprised by that. The Royal Bastards seemed to know everything. "Slightly stalker-ish."

"I know a lot about the things I take interest in," he replied.

"Is that so?" I countered.

"Get to work, pretty girl. I'll see you in a few hours." The line disconnected, and I was left alone in my office.

I dropped my phone on the desk and let out a scream. I was on the freaking roller coaster of emotions, and I was at the top of the hill. My heart was in my throat, and I didn't know what was going to happen next.

Whose life was I living? I prayed to God whoever's it was that they didn't want it back because I liked having Playboy around. My mind quickly snapped to reminding me Billie Jean was still missing.

And down the hill I went. My heart dropped, and a wave of worry washed over me. It had been a week since I had heard from her, and all we knew now was she had left with a strange guy. I hated that there wasn't anything for me to do. I didn't have a magic button that would bring Billie Jean back.

I still had the feeling she was alive. Whoever had taken her wasn't hurting her. At least, not yet. I held onto that feeling. It was my life raft, and I clung to it.

I grabbed a file I needed to start working on and knew I needed to focus on work or I would sit at my desk all day just worrying about Billie Jean.

There was four-ish more hours until Playboy showed up, and he could help distract me from worrying myself crazy over Billie Jean. Until then, I was going to bury myself in

work and just tell myself everything was going
to be okay.

It had to be.

*

Chapter Ten

Playboy

Afternoon delight…

I held my phone to my ear and wondered what the hell Sledge was calling me for. "Yo."

"Brother," he called.

I leaned against the bar. "Long time no talk, man. What the hell are you up to?" I asked.

Sledge and I had run in the same circles back when we were younger. He had called me a month or so ago asking about the Devil's Rebels and mentioned his new club was in a bit of hot water with them.

"Got a bit of a problem."

"More than the one you told me about before?"

Sledge groaned. "Same one, but it doesn't seem to be going anywhere."

"Oh, come on. I thought you guys were the Kings of Vengeance for a reason," I laughed.

"Yeah, we do vengeance pretty good around here, but we're coming up against some shit bigger than us."

The Devil's Rebels were bigger than most MCs. "What do you need from us?" I put the phone on speaker and laid it on the bar. Barracuda was sitting next to me, and it would be easier for him to hear whatever Sledge had to say straight from him. "You're on speaker and 'cuda can hear ya."

"Well, shit," Sledge grunted. "Let me grab Quinn. Might as well just have the two big dogs talking to each other."

There was some static and grumbling and then it cleared. "'Cuda," Quinn grunted into the phone.

"You got him," Barracuda replied.

"How are things going in Sacramento?" Quinn asked.

"Some shit happening, but nothing we can't handle. What do you having going on there? Seemed like you guys were handling your business pretty good the last time we talked," Barracuda grunted.

"Well, the thing of it is, when the Rolling Devils blew up, we sort of pissed off the Devil's Rebels more than we thought."

Oh. Shit. That was a club Royal Bastards tried to steer clear of.

"How so?" Barracuda asked.

"They got into the clubhouse and managed to kill one of the girl's cats. Now we have a demand for thirty grand or the deal they originally had with the Rolling Devils."

"And what was that?" I asked.

Quinn sighed, defeated. "Five girls initially and then three every month after."

I whistled low. Damn. That was a lot of money and trafficking humans was something no one should fuck with. Trafficking was a league only the scum tread in. "So, you give them thirty grand in hundreds?" I asked.

Barracuda chuckled.

"Well, we'd more than love to pay them the thirty, but we don't have it and the money tree we planted in the backyard isn't producing yet," Quinn grunted.

"So, tell me what you need, and I'll see what I can do to make shit happen for you." Barracuda paused. "It's gonna cost you, though."

"Never doubted that it would."

Barracuda pulled out his phone. "Let me set up a meeting with the Devils this coming week and see what I can work out."

"The sooner the better, but if it's gonna take a week, we get it."

"One of their head guys has a thing for one of the girls at the club. I'll get in touch with him today and get the ball rolling." Barracuda lowered his voice. "I can't promise you anything though, Quinn. I'm willing to try and help you, but we're not going to put our necks on the line to save you."

"Totally understand, Barracuda. We appreciate you just getting us in touch with them if that's all. Right now, we're at their mercy with this shitty burner phone they left after they broke in."

"Will do. Give us a bit of time, though. We're dealing with some shit right now."

"You got it, man," Quinn called. "We'll be waiting for your call."

I ended the call and tucked my phone in my back pocket.

"Are we really able to help them?" Sledge and I went way back, and he was a good guy. I didn't want to leave him hanging when we could help him out.

"I'd rather not, but we can put it to a vote, and I'll set up a meet with them before. If you guys are willing to put your necks on the line then I can't say no."

I didn't know if the other guys would want to help. "When are you calling church?"

Barracuda smirked. "I'll give ya a couple of days to try and convince some of the guys to get on your side."

I knew I wouldn't be able to convince all of the guys to help, but if I got the majority on my side then we would.

I glanced at the clock and saw it was getting close to noon.

"Where are you headed?" Barracuda asked.

I pulled my keys out of my pocket. "Got plans for lunch."

"Raelyn?"

"Yeah. How did things go with Leona last night?"

Barracuda shrugged. "About as well as you can expect with a drunk chick and a frozen pizza."

"Gotta say that's one scenario I've never been in before."

He held his glass up to me and smiled. "Maybe you should try it sometime, then."

Barracuda headed back to his room, and I walked to my bike. I had no clue what to get for lunch, but I needed to figure it out now.

I passed a Chinese place on the way to Raelyn's office and stopped to pick up two lunch specials. I had no idea what kind of food Raelyn liked, but I knew she wasn't picky. She tended to go with the flow.

I parked in front of her office and grabbed the food from my saddlebags.

The front door swung open, and Raelyn held it for me. "You're pretty punctual," she laughed.

I slipped in through the door but not without a swift kiss to her lips. "I said lunch and it's lunchtime, pretty girl."

She sighed lightly, and her cheeks flushed pink. "I like a man who keeps his word."

I stepped into the office and pushed my sunglasses on top of my head. "Small place," I murmured.

Raelyn laughed. "Yeah, it's cozy." She tipped her head toward the back of the office. "Follow me. I don't want you to get lost."

I followed her to her desk and set the bag of food down. "Thank God you didn't lose me. Things got confusing when we passed the coffee machine."

Raelyn laughed and moved a stack of papers to the side of her desk. "I see you're the smartass one now." She grabbed the bag and pulled everything out.

I sat in the chair opposite her and watched. "That's okay for lunch?"

Raelyn dropped the empty bag on the floor. "More than okay seeing as I didn't have to decide what to order."

"Guess I'll need to bring you lunch more often then." I looked around the office. "It's only you here?"

She nodded and handed me a plastic fork. "For today. Normally Leona is here with me."

I grabbed a container and snapped off the lid. "Is it really safe for you to be the only one here?"

She rolled her eyes. "Nothing is going to happen to me because no one ever really comes here besides my bosses. Who, by the way, I haven't seen in three weeks. They tend to stay on the job site while Leona and I handle all of the boring contracts and paperwork."

The phone on the desk rang, and she picked it up.

I had never had a real nine-to-five job before, and I sat back to watch Raelyn in her element. She listened for a second and then turned to her computer. She started talking about floating decks and the price of using real wood and some fake shit that she swore looked just like real wood.

I was halfway done with my food before she finally got off the phone after telling the person on the other end of the phone that they wouldn't regret going with the fake shit.

"You like your job?"

Raelyn laughed and dug into her food. "I like that it pays my bills."

"You seem pretty damn good at it."

She finished chewing and smiled. "Talking clients off the ledge seems to be my specialty. Leona tends to throw all the crazy calls my way so I've learned how to deal with them pretty well." She stood up and walked over to the small fridge. "Did you want something to drink?" she called.

I nodded. "Whatever you got is good."

She grabbed two bottles of water and handed one to me. "Sorry, no beer," she laughed.

"If there was, I might consider working here if you and Leona drink while you help plan people's dream houses."

She plopped back in her chair. "I'll be sure to let Boomer and Post know they could get more employees if they offered an open bar."

"Pretty sure people would love to go to work if open bars were available."

"Definitely would make work more interesting."

We chatted while we finished eating, and I couldn't help but notice how easily Raelyn and I seemed to be with each other. Whether we were talking about her job, her sister, Leona, or the fact Leona hadn't come home last night, I was fully engaged and hanging on her every word.

"I'm pretty sure Leona was still holed up with Barracuda when I left."

"Shut up," Raelyn gasped. She grabbed our empty containers and dropped them in the trash. "Also, I can't believe you didn't tell me Leona never made it home when I texted you."

I shrugged and snagged her by the hand when she walked past me. "I didn't want to worry you on top of everything else. I knew she was in good hands with Barracuda." I pulled her to me and into my lap.

She laughed and wound her arms around my neck. "I've never had the pleasure of sitting like this at work before."

I brushed her hair behind her ear. "It's been too long since I kissed you, and I saw my opening."

"Is that so?" she whispered.

I nodded. "It is, pretty girl."

Her lips hovered over mine. "So, are you going to kiss me, then?"

"Don't gotta ask me twice, pretty girl." I closed the gap between us, and her fingers delved into my hair. She moaned under my kiss, and she plastered her body against mine.

The kiss went wild.

My hands roamed over her back and tugged the hem of her shirt up. I touched the warm, bare skin of her back and growled. "You're perfect, Raelyn."

She mewled into my mouth and dug her fingers into my hair. She twisted in my arms and straddled my waist.

There was no stopping this kiss. We had only known each other a short time, but the sexual tension that had built between us was more than either of us could take anymore.

I bunched her shirt up and pulled it over her head.

"Playboy," she gasped.

"No one comes in here, right?" I growled.

She shook her head but looked around unsure.

I stood, her lush body in my arms, and stalked to the front door. I was going to make Raelyn mine. Nothing was going to stop me.

I twisted the lock on the door. "Better?"

She bit her bottom lip and nodded. "Much better." I strode over to the closest desk and cleared everything off it with a sweep of my hand. I sat her ass on the edge, and my fingers went to the button of her pants.

I popped it open and slid the zipper down.

"We're really doing this here?" she panted.

My eyes connected with hers. "Nothing is going to stop me unless you tell me no."

"Not saying no. Just needed a second to get some oxygen back to my brain." A wonky smile spread across her lips.

"Got enough oxygen now?"

She grabbed a fistful of my shirt and pulled me close. "Oxygen is overrated." She plastered her lips to mine, and I growled into her mouth. Her tongue moved against mine, and she grabbed my shirt. She ripped it off and tossed it on the floor. Her hands went to the fly of my jeans and clawed to pop open the button.

I brushed her hands away and had my pants open within seconds. She pushed them down my legs and gasped when her eyes found my dick bobbing between them. She pressed a hand to my chest and pushed me back. My pants were around my ankles.

She dropped to her knees in front of me. "Holy fuck." She tipped her head back and looked up at me. "This is mine."

Whatever she wanted, she could fucking have.

Her hand wrapped around my dick, and she stroked slowly.

My sweet little Raelyn had turned into a vixen who had eyes only for my dick. I didn't know where she had learned her moves, but I was fucking thankful she knew them.

Her lips wrapped around my cock, and her tongue swirled over the tip.

I delved my fingers into her hair and watched as her head bobbed up and down. One hand stayed at the base of my cock and the other laid in her lap.

"Touch yourself," I ordered. I wanted my cock in her mouth and her fingers in her pussy.

Her eyes opened, and she stared up at me as my cock slowly slid down her throat. Her hand moved from her thigh and crept into her open pants. She raised up, her knees still on the floor, but her hand now on her pussy.

"Are you wet for me, baby?" I asked.

She moaned on my dick.

"Stroke that clit. Imagine it's my tongue."

She wasn't going to have to imagine for long. She had about thirty seconds before I picked her up and laid her out on the desk so I could devour her.

A gasp escaped her lips, and I slipped my dick further down her throat. She gagged slightly but didn't move her head back. Her eyes connected with mine, and she swallowed around my cock.

"Holy shit," I groaned.

She swallowed again, and I was seconds from coming down her throat.

I grabbed her under her arms and lifted her up and onto the desk in one swoop. I pushed her legs up so her heels rested on the desk and she was spread wide for me. I devoured her pussy. The sweet taste coated my tongue as her fingers delved into my hair and she held me in place.

"Oh, my God," she moaned. "God, yes!"

I sucked her clit into my mouth and swirled my tongue around it. Her hips bucked up, pressing her pussy into my face, and I dug in deeper.

Raelyn's pleasure was the only thing I wanted. Her moans and pants of desire spurred me on until she cried out. "Playboy!" she yelled. "I'm coming!"

Her already wet pussy flooded around me, and I lapped at her clit with short, firm strokes with my tongue. She chanted my name, her orgasm crashing around her. Her body slowly relaxed until her ass was finally back on the desk, and her fingers eased in my hair.

I leaned back and wiped my face with the back of my hand. "Ready for more, pretty girl?"

She closed her eyes and bit her lip. "There's more?" she whispered.

"We're just getting started."

*

Raelyn

I was going to die right then and there.

Playboy's mouth on me was more than I had ever felt before.

When he had dropped his pants, I couldn't control myself. I needed to know what he tasted like and nothing was going to stop me from finding out.

The salty taste of his dick lingered in my mouth, and I wanted more. I just wasn't sure I could take more after that Earth-shattering orgasm.

Playboy crouched down for a second and popped back up with a condom in his hand. He raised it to his mouth and tore off the corner with his teeth. "Been wanting to fuck you since the night you knocked on my door, pretty girl. I know what your mouth feels like around my dick, but now I need to know what that pussy feels like."

He rolled the condom onto his cock, and I just watched. Playboy was a beautiful sight that begged to not only be looked at but also touched. I could spend hours exploring him visually and touching him, and I knew it wouldn't be enough.

He grabbed my hips and scooted me to the very edge of the desk. I sat up, wrapped my arms around his neck, and he nestled between my legs. He took off my glasses, folded them, and set them on the desk. Thank goodness I could still see somewhat without them.

"As much as I want this to last forever, pretty girl, I'm gonna fuck you hard and quick because I'm about ten seconds from coming all over you."

I was happy with whatever he gave me.

Hard and fast.

Sweet and soft.

I would take it all and want more.

He pressed a hard kiss to my lips, and I reached down between us. I wrapped my fingers around his cock and squeezed. "I want whatever you will give me."

I was desperate for him, and I wasn't ashamed to admit it.

His fingers delved into my hair, and his hand gripped the back of my head. "Put my dick inside you," he ordered.

I watched as I guided his dick inside me and gasped when his other hand grabbed my waist and held me there. He tugged my hair and tipped my head back 'til my eyes connected with his.

"You feel that?' he growled.

I mewled in response, unable to string two words together.

"That's me, pretty girl. Ain't no one ever gonna be here again except for me. You got that?"

I nodded stiffly. "Yes, Playboy."

He had claimed me, and I loved it.

He wanted to own me? I was his to take. Nothing had ever felt more right.

Inch by sweet inch, he slowly pulled back then slammed back into me. "Who do you belong to?" he grunted.

He pulled back out and plunged back in before I could get the words out.

"Who do you belong to?" he demanded again. "Say it," he growled.

"You," I gasped. He pulled out and slammed back in. "I belong to you, Playboy."

His lips crashed down on mine, and he claimed my mouth the same way he had claimed my pussy. His hips moved into me, and I arched up to meet his thrusts.

This was what I had wanted. The second I had met Playboy, I knew if I was lucky enough to be able to touch this man, I would never be the same.

My second orgasm built with each thrust, promising to be even better than the one his mouth had given me.

Playboy had been made for me, and I never wanted to give him up. Giving up this feeling was something I never would be able to do.

His hand at my hip grazed over my skin and found my clit. His thumb glided over the tight bud.

One flick.

Two flicks.

My orgasm crashed over me just as Playboy shouted my name and thrust one last time. He clutched me close, and I felt his dick throb inside me.

"Fucking best," he gasped.

I closed my eyes and submerged myself in the feeling. Playboy held me close, and I buried my face in his chest.

We both panted, trying to catch our breaths.

His hands rubbed over my back, and my body slowly drifted down from pure ecstasy.

"Now that's what I call a lunch break." Playboy chuckled, and his body rumbled against me.

"If this is what happens when Leona calls in sick, I hope she never comes back," I mumbled.

Playboy leaned back, and a satisfied smile played on his lips. "You get that open bar and Leona will be out of a job."

I sighed and reached up. I traced a finger over his perfect lips. "I'm pretty sure if you took Leona's job, nothing would ever get done and we would both get fired."

He shrugged and pressed a quick kiss to my lips. "But what fun we would have before we got fired."

The phone rang next to my ass, and I instinctively answered it without blinking. "Holmes and Gains Construction." Yes, I had just answered the phone with Playboy's dick still inside me.

Playboy smothered a laugh with the back of his hand, and I glared at him.

"Sure. I'm right by your desk. I'll make sure it's there." I dropped the phone back on the cradle, fumbled to get my glasses back on, and leaned over to look at the papers on the floor.

"Who was that?" Playboy asked.

"Leona," I mumbled. "She asked me to make sure the Trent file was on her desk."

Playboy looked down. "Uh, is it somewhere down there?"

I shrugged. "Let's hope so." I looked up at him and smiled. "Also, this is Leona's desk."

Whoops.

*

Chapter Eleven

Playboy

Roll the tape…

"What are we going to do to help them?"

I shrugged and pulled out a cigarette. "We've got the money to help them."

"You really think just giving the Devil's Rebels the money they want is going to make them go away?" Tank asked. "They'll find some bullshit reason to demand more six months from now. Once you fuck with the Devil's Rebels, you might as well just accept the fact you'll forever owe them."

Tank was probably more than right.

"But it would keep them happy for a while," Jet pointed out.

"So, we lend the Kings the money, but what are we really getting out of it?" Six-Gun asked.

We were gathered around the bar, and I was trying to persuade the guys to help the Kings of Vengeance. It was going as well as I had anticipated.

Not well.

"Interest on the loan," I suggested.

Barracuda walked into the common room and pulled up a stool. "They want in on Skinz," he stated.

Rebel scoffed. "Say what?"

Barracuda shrugged. "They want to buy into the franchise. We let them use the clout of the name and then take a skim off of their profits. We also charge interest on the thirty K loan."

Skinz had over ten clubs along the west coast. It was a very profitable business because of the high standards we had when it came to the girls and the atmosphere of the club. The club just down the road from the clubhouse was the first one we had opened, and it was our most profitable. Deciding to expand the Skinz club with a different MC at the helm was risky, but it could also make us a lot of money.

"If we let them use the name, this could become something bigger. We could become a franchise that people could pay big bucks to buy into," Monk pointed out.

Barracuda nodded. "It definitely has big potential if we do it right. I'm gonna run the idea through a couple of the other presidents of other Royal Bastards chapters, though. I need an outside perspective to see if it really is a good idea."

The guys agreed if other chapters thought it was a good idea then it was something they wanted to move forward with.

"You two manage to go over the tapes from the club?" Barracuda asked Rebel and Tank.

Tank nodded. "Yeah. We figured out which guy Violet was talking about. He showed up at ten and stayed until close."

"He was outside in his car when Billie Jean walked out." Rebel grabbed a beer and popped the top.

"He grabbed her?" I asked.

Tank shook his head. "Nope. She walked right up to his car, got in, and then they drove off."

"What the fuck?" Barracuda grumbled. "That doesn't make any fucking sense. As far as we know, Billie Jean never saw the guy in her life before and she just drives off with him?"

"But that wasn't the last time we caught him on camera, though." Rebel pulled out his phone and handed it to Barracuda. "That is from the last shift Memphis worked."

I shifted behind Barracuda and watched the clip of the film on his phone. "That's the same guy."

"Sure the fuck is." Tank pointed at the phone. "Keep watching."

"Guy sat in Memphis' section the whole night. Doesn't talk to her too much or seem suspicious. Stays until close. Goes out to his car and waits. Memphis walks out of the club, gets in his car, and they drive off." Rebel shook his head.

"What the fuck?" Barracuda growled. "Why the fuck do they get in the car with him?" he demanded.

I grabbed the phone from Barracuda and watched the video of Memphis again. None of this was making sense. The connection between Billie Jean and Memphis was this guy, but I was fucking stumped as to why and what happened.

"You think he's somehow getting the girl's to come home with him and then he's killing them?" Jet asked.

"We got a fucking serial killer on our hands?" Jinx suggested.

"Whatever the fuck is going on, we need to get that guy's picture in the hands of all of the girls. If he's managed to grab two girls already, there's no way to know if he's looking to take more girls." He pointed at the phone. "Get the best picture of him that you can and circulate it with everyone at the club. Double the security at the door, and let's see if we can catch this guy."

Tank nodded. "Will do, 'cuda."

"Someone has to know who this guy is, and we're gonna fucking find out." Barracuda slammed his fist on the bar.

Whoever this guy was, he was fucking with the girls at the club, and that meant he was fucking with the club.

I pulled my phone out and sent a text to Raelyn. Yesterday, when we had lunch and tested out Leona's desk, we hadn't talked about what was happening with Billie Jean. I could tell she was struggling with not knowing what was going on. I had been trying to figure out what happened that night but was coming up short. Now we at least had a picture of one of the last people to be seen with Billie Jean.

Coming over for dinner. Got some news.

Raelyn was just getting off work, and I knew she was going to want to know anything I did right away.

The sooner we got the Billie Jean and Memphis mystery solved, the sooner I could focus fully on Raelyn.

Right now, whatever was going on between us was a good distraction, but I wanted us to be more than just a distraction.

I wanted a whole hell of a lot more than that from her. I wanted all of her attention, and the only way I was going to get that was to find her sister and bring her home.

Time to kick this shit into high gear and be the hero Raelyn had been looking for when she knocked on my door.

*

Chapter Twelve

Raelyn

I'll show you patronizing…

"So they both left willingly?" I asked.

Playboy nodded and grabbed a hamburger off the tray. "At least, that is what it looks like on the surveillance video." He squirted ketchup and mayo on the burger and slapped the top bun on. "Neither Billie Jean nor Memphis looked like they were forced to leave with him."

"But why?" I had asked the same question four times already. None of this made sense. Not one bit of it. "Why is he taking the girls? Why Billie Jean and Memphis?"

There were tons of girls who worked at the club, yet he had targeted those two.

"If we knew why, we wouldn't be sitting here." Playboy took a huge bite of his burger. "The only good thing that has come out of this is you and me," he muttered around a mouthful.

"You and me?" I asked.

Playboy took a drink of his beer and swallowed. "Yeah, pretty girl. I doubt you would have ever made it to the clubhouse if this wouldn't have happened."

I rolled my eyes. "Are you telling me you don't think I'm the biker chick type?" I wasn't. Not at all. Unless it was Playboy.

He wiped his mouth with the back of his hand and chuckled. "I think you are now."

I flitted my hand in the air. "Let's focus on Billie Jean right now. What do we do next?"

"We're gonna get the guy's picture in everyone's hands at the club. We're hoping that might help spark a memory in one of the girls."

My mind was racing with every possible thought of who the guy could be.

Why would Billie Jean get in the car with him? Billie Jean wasn't into guys at all so it wasn't like she went home with him to hookup.

"What's got your brow furrowed, pretty girl?" He reached out and pressed a finger to my brow.

"I just don't know what to think, Playboy. Why would she get in the car with him? Why is she gone?"

Playboy sighed. "I know you two are close, Raelyn, but maybe you don't know your sister as well as you think you do."

I leaned away from his touch. "What does that mean?"

"It means she maybe into things that you have no idea about."

What was he talking about? He was talking around what he really wanted to say. "I think you need to just come out and say whatever it is you're dancing around."

Playboy sighed heavily. "I see a lot of things at the club, pretty girl. I've never seen Billie Jean take drugs, but she may just be good at hiding it."

"You think she went with that guy to get drugs or something?" Nope. That wasn't it. I knew it wasn't.

"It's a possibility that can't be ruled out. I know Memphis had some problems last year," he trailed off.

I shook my head. "So that means Billie Jean had the same problem? No. Billie Jean wouldn't do drugs. You obviously don't know her at all. She may dress sexy and tough and have an attitude, but she would never do drugs. She would tell you straight to your face you were an idiot if you touched drugs."

Playboy held up his hands. "I'm just talking here, Raelyn. You can't rule out a possibility without exploring it."

"But it doesn't sound like you're exploring it at all. It sounds like you decided that's what is going on." I shook my head. "I'm not going to believe what you're saying unless I see the proof. There are so many other possibilities of why she left with that guy."

"You need to take a breath and calm down, pretty girl."

I shook my head. Yeah, no. Don't tell me to calm down. Playboy didn't have anything invested in Billie Jean. He wasn't close to her. She wasn't his damn sister. "I don't need to take a breath," I hissed. "I need to find my sister and bring her home."

Playboy stepped toward me, but I held my hand out.

"Raelyn. I'm here to help you," he reasoned.

I shook my head. "But are you? Somehow, I got lost in you, and now, I'm not doing enough to find Billie Jean. She's been gone for over a week," I wailed. "What am I doing while my sister is God knows where and probably being treated like shit? I'm sitting in my house, eating good food, and talking to you. How is that me doing everything I can to find her?" I demanded.

Somehow, I had gotten tangled up with Playboy and had gotten distracted from what I needed him for.

Playboy grabbed my arm and tried to pull me toward him. "Raelyn," he cooed. "I'm not telling you to calm down and forget about your sister."

I dug my heels in and didn't move. "I should be losing sleep. Out on the streets looking for her. Hell, I should have gone to the police. I just assumed they would ignore me, but will they?" I ranted. I ran my fingers through my hair, pulled off my glasses, and rubbed at my eyes.

My feelings had been on a roller coaster the past week, and I was in a deep valley right now. There didn't seem to be any way up.

Playboy dropped my hand and closed the distance between us. "Keep talking, pretty girl. Let it all out." He wrapped me in his arms and held me tight.

"I just don't know what to do, Playboy. It feels wrong that I'm here with you, but where else should I be? I don't know anything other than I need to find Billie Jean." It felt right being with Playboy, but was this the right time for it? "I'm the happiest I've ever been when I'm with you, but then this is also the worst time of my life. How do I find you when the world I knew is crashing down around me?"

Playboy shifted his fingers through my hair. "Because you were supposed to have me right now, Raelyn. I'm here to keep you up. I'm here to be the person you can lean on. I'm here because this is where I'm meant to be."

I closed my eyes and sighed. So many emotions rolled through me at any given time. Happy one second and the next overcome by despair. "I need to find Billie Jean," I whispered.

"We will, pretty girl. We're getting closer. I know it doesn't feel like it, but we are. We know she left with someone, and it doesn't look like he forced her to leave with him. She was safe the last time we saw her."

I buried my face in Playboy's chest. He was being nice. He was being there for me through my breakdown. He was listening when half of what I said probably didn't make sense.

He was just there for me.

"Billie Jean swore up and down she would never do drugs, Playboy, but maybe something changed. Maybe you're right." I couldn't turn away from the possibility. Maybe Billie Jean had gotten into some trouble and she turned to drugs. Right now, I had to consider every possibility.

"Or maybe I'm wrong. We just have to keep our minds open to everything, yeah?"

I nodded. "Yeah."

"And, it's okay to feel everything you are, pretty girl. You didn't knock on my door with the intention of hooking up with me."

I scoffed. "Uh, well, we did agree you would help me and you could do whatever you wanted to me."

Playboy laughed. "You were gonna be mine either way, pretty girl. You saying I could have my way with you just showed me you were more than willing."

"I was lucky you didn't laugh in my face and shove me out the door."

He ran his hand down my back. "I would have been a damn fool if I did that."

"I thought I had a little bit of a chance with you seeing how your name is Playboy. Show a little leg and get you to help me." I busted out laughing and Playboy sputtered.

"Uh, showed a little leg? You had on a damn sweatshirt that was two sizes too big and jeans, pretty girl. I had to use my damn imagination to figure out what you looked like under all of those clothes."

"Well, you know. It was my intention to show a little leg," I mumbled.

"You're a damn nut, Raelyn," he chuckled.

And back up the roller coaster I went. When Playboy was around, I wasn't down for long. "I'm normally even keeled," I whispered.

"I'm sure you are," Playboy agreed.

I leaned back and looked up at him. "That sounded like you were patronizing me."

He raised an eyebrow. "Did it?"

I rolled my eyes and pulled out of his arms. "Well, now that I had my breakdown, we can get back to eating, yeah?"

Playboy ran his fingers through his hair. "Whatever you want, pretty girl."

I grabbed a plate and set a cheeseburger on it. "Totally patronizing me," I laughed.

"I'll show you patronizing later, Raelyn." He grabbed his plate and winked.

My heartbeat doubled, and my cheeks heated. At the peak of the roller coaster and Playboy was always there.

Through the highs and lows, he stayed.

That was something I never expected.

Not in a million years.

*

Playboy

"Do it again."

I moaned and slowly glided out. "Your pussy is like a fucking vise."

Raelyn bucked her hips up as I came back down. "It's your fault," she gasped. "You're so…ah…big."

Her words spurred me on. I grabbed her wrists and pinned them to the bed over her head. "You better be ready to fucking come, pretty girl."

She bit her lip as I bottomed out inside her. "Fuck me harder," she gasped. "Fuck me, Playboy."

I reared back, grabbed her around the waist, and flipped her over. "Knees up, ass in the air," I ordered.

She got her knees under her and buried her face in the mattress. I ran my hand over the dip in her back. "Love this fucking ass." I grabbed a handful of her ass and squeezed.

She moaned and pushed back into me. "Fuck me," she moaned.

I plunged back inside her and moaned. Raelyn's pussy was heaven. I could die a happy man right then and there. Raelyn was where I needed to be.

With each thrust, she reared back, meeting me. My name fell from her lips, pleading for me to never stop.

A guttural scream ripped from her mouth, and her body tensed. Her pussy milked my cock, and I came right along with her orgasm.

I fell to the side, my cum deep inside her, and gathered her in my arms. I pulled the covers haphazardly over us and tried to catch my breath.

"I like that," she gasped.

"I aim to please, pretty girl."

She held her thumb up in the air. "Two enthusiastic yet exhausted thumbs up."

I chuckled and pressed a kiss to her neck. "I'm staying the night," I whispered.

She hummed and patted my arm. "You bet your ass you are."

I rolled to my back, turned off the light, and twisted back to Raelyn. She sighed heavily and relaxed into me.

She was asleep within seconds—her breathing even and her warm body in my arms.

This is where I was always meant to be.

Raelyn was what I needed, and I was never going to let her go.

*

Chapter Thirteen

Raelyn

OH. MY. GOD.

"I'll be over later."

I glanced at the clock. It has half past ten. At night. "Um, okay?" Didn't get much later than that.

Playboy laughed into the phone. "I'm doing security at the club tonight. I tried to get out of it, but Barracuda was being a dick. I'm supposed to stay until close, but I'm hoping I can make sure shit is running smooth, put some prospects at the doors, and get the hell out of here."

Playboy had texted me earlier that he would be over after dinner but that obviously wasn't going to happen. Work had been quiet, and there hadn't been any word on finding the guy who was with Billie Jean. I tried to keep my calm and remind myself I was going to find her. She was still alive. I could feel it.

"Call me when you get here. I'll unlock the door for you."

"I shouldn't be too much longer." The loud music from the club sounded in the background.

"Are you out smoking?" I laughed.

"Yeah."

I rolled my eyes. "You need to quit."

"You were the one who told me it was sexy."

I groaned. I had. This morning I had followed him out to his bike to say goodbye, and he had lit up before leaving. I had been so mesmerized watching him light the cigarette and blow out a plume of smoke that the words might have slipped from my mouth before I realized.

"Anything you do tends to be sexy," I muttered. That was the damn truth. Playboy just standing there breathing was enough to get me hot and bothered.

"Same goes for you, pretty girl. Even when you're having a breakdown, I can't help but think how beautiful you are."

His words warmed my heart, and I sighed. "Are you sure you can't leave right now?"

He chuckled. "I wish I could. Lock the doors, hit the bed, and I'll call you when I'm at the door."

"Bye, handsome." I ended the call and tossed my phone on the bed.

I had been hoping Playboy would have been over a lot sooner, but at least he was coming. I flipped off the light and slipped under the covers.

I missed having Playboy in bed with me.

How quickly I had gotten used to having him around. Life had changed as I knew it, and I prayed to God that after we found Billie Jean that things wouldn't go back to normal.

Normal was no Playboy.

I didn't want normal anymore.

I wanted Playboy.

*

I blindly reached for my phone and put it to my ear. "Hmm? Are you here?"

"Raelyn?"

My eyes popped open, and I jackknifed up. "Billie Jean?" Oh, my God. OH, MY GOD!

"It's me, Rae."

"Where are you? What happened to you? Tell me where you are. I'm coming to get you," I ranted. I threw back the covers and jumped out of bed with my phone pressed to my ear.

"I only have like a minute, Rae. Shut up and let me talk," she whispered. Her voice was raspy, and I stopped in my tracks.

"Talk to me, Billie."

"I messed up, Rae. I got into some trouble, and I can't get out of it."

Oh, my God. "Tell me how to help. I'll do anything you need."

"You can't help. This is bigger than you and me. I need you to go to the Royal Bastards clubhouse. They're the only ones who are going to be able to help me."

"And tell them what?" I demanded. Billie Jean said she didn't have much time to talk. I needed to get as much information from her as I could. I could tell her after she was back home that I already went to them before she told me to go there. "Where are you?"

"I don't know. I'm here with another girl from the club, Memphis. I managed to smuggle my phone down here with me and hide it. Thanks to you bugging me to always have a portable charger with me, I was able to keep my phone on."

She was with Memphis. They were both okay. At least, for now. "What am I supposed to tell the Royal Bastards?" I could rub it in her face when she was back home that I was right about always carrying a charger with her.

"Tell them I got in deep with Jester. I'm in a basement somewhere. They've kept us drugged, and today was the first day I've been able to open my eyes for more than a five minutes."

"How are we supposed to find you, Billie Jean?" She was in a basement somewhere. Playboy was going to need a hell of a lot more details than that.

"I don't know," she whispered. "I saw one guy had a cut on it that said Devil's Rebel. Just tell them that, Raelyn. I wish I had more to tell them, but that's all I have."

"Who took you?"

"Mac. Memphis and I are beat up pretty bad, but we're fine for now. But we need to get out of here, Raelyn. I don't know what they plan on doing with us."

Who in the hell were Jester and Mac? Playboy had been right. There were things about Billie Jean I didn't know. "I'll tell th—"

Billie Jean gasped. "Shit." The line went dead.

"Billie Jean!" I hollered. "Billie!"

Oh shit. Something happened. Had whoever took her found out she had been on the phone?

My phone rang in my hand, and I jumped. I dropped the phone on the floor and fell to the hard wood in the dark. I felt around under the bed and grabbed the phone. Playboy's name flashed on the screen. I swiped right and pressed the phone to my ear. "She called me!" I shouted.

"Raelyn?" he called, confused. "Who called you?"

"Billie Jean! She just called me."

"Holy fuck," Playboy cussed. "I'm at your door. Let me in."

I jumped up and flew down the hall. I fumbled with the lock and finally threw open the door. "She got in trouble with Jester, and she saw a guy with the Devil's Rebels cut. Mac took her." I had to tell Playboy before I forgot what Billie Jean had told me.

Playboy planted a hand on my stomach and pushed me into the house. He closed the door behind him and locked it.

"We have to go, Playboy. Now." I tried to push him out of the way, but he wrapped his arm around me.

"Go where?" he asked.

Uh, well. "I don't know, but we need to go. I think someone figured out she was on the phone. She hung up in the middle of my talking. Let me go," I demanded.

"Calm, Raelyn." He guided me into the living room and pushed me onto the couch. "Start from the beginning and don't forget anything."

I rattled off that I had been sleeping and answered the phone thinking it was just him calling to let him in. I tried to tell him word for word what Billie Jean had said. At least I remembered the important parts.

"Fucking shit," he muttered when I was done.

"So, now we need to go." I tried to get up, but he held me down. "Playboy," I shouted. What in the hell was he doing? This is what we had been waiting for.

He pulled his phone out of his pocket. He swiped a few times and then there was a loud ring. He was calling someone.

The phone rang three times.

"What in the fuck are you calling me for?" Barracuda did not sound happy.

"Who is that?" a woman called in the background.

"Leona!" I gasped.

Leona shrieked.

Holy cow. Tonight was full of surprises. I had been trying to get out of Leona what had happened with Barracuda, but she was like a steel trap. Not telling me a single thing. Obviously, things had worked out pretty well seeing as she was with him in the middle of the night.

"Quiet, woman," Barracuda grunted. "What the fuck are you calling me for, Playboy?"

"Billie Jean just called Raelyn," Playboy replied.

"Holy fuck. Hell of a time to call."

I agreed, but I was just happy she had called me finally. I hadn't heard my sister's voice in over a week.

"She doesn't know where she is but—"

"But she said she messed up and got in deep with Chester. Mac took her."

"Jester," Playboy corrected me.

Whoops. "Jester. And she doesn't know where she is but she saw a guy with a Double Rebels cut thing on."

"Devil's Rebels," Playboy corrected me again.

"For Pete's sake, woman. Try to get the details right," Barracuda grunted.

I was just a tad bit excited.

"You're doing great, Raelyn," Leona called.

"Anything else?" Barracuda asked.

I shook my head.

Playboy smirked at me. "No," he said out loud.

"This is a lot of shit to pile on me at two o'clock in the morning." Barracuda sighed. "Get your ass here in the morning, and we'll try to make heads and tails of all of this. We're gonna have to see if we can find Jester and figure out who the hell Mac was. I'm assuming neither of them are going to be easy to find."

"Oh," I interrupted. "She said she was fine right now but she didn't know for how long that would be."

"We'll find him. You and I both know that fucker can't stay hidden forever." Playboy reached out and laced his fingers through mine.

"True. Get some sleep, and we'll get this shit sorted tomorrow." The call ended, and Playboy tossed his phone on the coffee table.

"That's it?" I asked. "We're not doing anything?"

We needed to go now. Barracuda needed to get his butt out of bed and gather the troops. This is what we had been waiting for and nothing was going to happen until morning? Adrenaline coursed through my veins. *Let's go!*

"It's the middle of the night, Raelyn. We gotta at least wait until the sun rises."

But what if something happened to Billie Jean before then? "It sounded like someone walked in on her when I was talking. She ended the call quickly."

"She told you she was fine, right?"

I nodded.

"So if she's fine now, we can at least wait until the sun rises," Playboy reasoned.

"How am I supposed to wait?" I demanded.

"It's the middle of the night, Raelyn. You need to get some sleep so you're ready for tomorrow."

"It's tomorrow right now," I countered.

Playboy ran his fingers through his hair. He looked tired. Really tired. "Raelyn," he groaned.

I folded my arms over my chest. "Fine. You can sleep."

"We're both going to sleep."

Fat chance of that. No way I was going to be able to sleep now. "You go to bed. I'll just wait."

"For what?"

"The sun to rise."

Playboy shook his head. "You're a nut." He stood up, leaned over me, pushed me back into the couch, and then lifted me up into his arms. "You don't have to sleep, but you're gonna be next to me while I sleep."

"That's ridiculous," I protested.

"So is staying awake all night," he countered. He flipped off the lights on the way to the bedroom, and I crossed my arms over my chest. I was not happy having to go to bed after finding out Billie Jean was in trouble. He was right about us not being able to do much now, but going to sleep didn't seem like the right thing either.

He laid me in the middle of the bed and pulled the covers over me. "Stay." He walked into the bathroom, and I flopped back on the bed.

A minute later, the toilet flushed, the water in the sink ran, he flipped off the light, and then he was in bed with me.

"I'm not happy about this." I needed to say it out loud. I was sure he could figure that out, but I wanted it to be perfectly clear.

"Got that, pretty girl." He gathered me in his arms, and I laid my head on his chest. "Just try to keep still so I can get a couple hours of shuteye before you take off in the sunrise to rescue your sister."

"You get two hours. That's it." No more.

Playboy lightly stroked my bare arm and hummed softly. "Stop talking."

I scoffed. "How rude."

"You want me to be rested to rescue your sister or dead on my feet? It was a long night at the club tonight, Raelyn. All I wanted to do was fall into bed with you and sleep until noon." He grunted and pulled me close. "Now I'll be lucky if you let me sleep past six."

Well. I guess I could shut up and let him sleep. "Sorry," I muttered.

"You're fine, Raelyn. I know you're excited. Just give me two hours, yeah?"

"Yeah," I whispered. I settled into his arms and listened to the sound of his breathing.

I had thought I wouldn't be able to sleep but with the dark room, Playboy pressed against me, and the soothing sound of his steady breaths, I drifted off within minutes.

Billie Jean may not be home yet, but just knowing that she was still alive and I had talked to her gave me a sense of relief. We were far from being past all of this, but I knew the end was in sight.

It had felt like ages since I had seen Billie Jean, but I knew she would be back soon.

I slept better than I had in over a week.

Billie Jean was coming home.

*

Chapter Fourteen

Playboy

A different world…

"What is this?"

Raelyn handed me a black thermos. "Coffee. We don't have time to sit here and drink it."

I grabbed the thermos. "Pretty girl, you're starting to be crazy again."

She rolled her eyes and grabbed her keys off the counter. "You know that it's seven-thirty, right? I let you sleep way longer than I said I would."

Five hours. Not exactly the desired amount I had in mind when I pulled into her driveway last night. And for the record, I had woken up before Raelyn.

Raelyn stood by the front door and tapped her foot.

I grabbed my sunglasses off the kitchen counter and pulled my keys out of my pocket. "We're taking the bike."

"Fine. But I need my keys to get back in the house."

I grabbed her keys and shoved them in my pocket. "Once this shit is over, you're giving me a copy of your key."

She opened the door and motioned for me to move. "Fine by me." She pulled the door shut behind us, locked it, and stalked over to my bike.

"I see you're hopped up on adrenaline again." I threw my leg over the bike, and she was on behind me before I set my ass down.

"I don't know what you're talking about," she muttered.

I handed her the thermos. "Hold that since you won't let me enjoy my coffee."

She grabbed the thermos and wedged it between us. "Drive, biker man."

I rolled my eyes and pulled my sunglasses over them. "You know, you could be a little nicer to me this morning."

She wrapped her arms around me and rested her chin on my shoulder. "Sorry," she whispered. "Apparently adrenaline puts me on edge a touch."

"Just a touch," I laughed. I cranked the bike up, walked it back, and pulled out of the driveway.

We were at the clubhouse ten minutes later, and Raelyn clamored to get off the bike. I grabbed her hand before she ran in guns blazing.

"Playboy," she protested. "Would you let me go?"

I wrapped her in my arms and pulled her close. "Gotta talk to you for a second, pretty girl."

She growled and bared her teeth.

"Walking through that door is a whole different world, you get me? You can't talk to Barracuda like you are to me." She was pushing her luck with me, but I cared about Raelyn. I understood she was feeling a lot of shit right now.

Barracuda was not going to be as understanding.

"We have to get to Billie Jean," she insisted.

"And we will," I reassured her. "But you gotta understand that when we walk through that door, Barracuda is calling the shots and you might not be a part of everything."

"What are you talking about? She's my sister. Of course I'll be a part of everything."

Jesus. Raelyn was not going to like what I had to say. "We walk in there, and Barracuda calls church. Your ass is not going to be able to sit with me."

"That's crazy, Playboy. She called *me.* She talked to *me.*"

"You're right, pretty girl, but you need the Royal Bastards and you're not part of the club. You've been lucky to hear things that most people never would. That night at the club when Barracuda sat around with you and Leona? That shit *rarely* ever happens. I know you think it's all talk, but I mean it when I say walking through those doors is a different world from the one you live in."

"I need to know what is happening, Playboy. She's my sister," Raelyn pleaded.

I ran my fingers through my hair. "The men your sister is roped into are not good, Raelyn. They don't think twice before killing someone."

The Royal Bastards were the same. That was the reason why Billie Jean had told Raelyn to get us. She understood the type of world she was in and knew the only way out was to bring in the Bastards.

"You're scaring me, Playboy." Her eyes were large, and she bit her bottom lip.

Good. That was going to be the thing for her to slow her roll and let the Royal Bastards handle things. "Take my lead on this, Raelyn. You're gonna have to trust me and believe that I'm going to do everything I can get to get Billie Jean, okay?"

She sighed and nodded. "Fine. But I don't like the fact you're gonna boot me from the room because I'm not part of the club."

"Ask any MC, pretty girl, and they'll laugh in your face if you ask them to sit in on church."

She rolled her eyes. "Whatever. This is going to be the only time where I'm gonna be involved in stuff like this. You get Billie Jean back, and I'm gonna make her sit her ass home to knit scarves and baby booties."

I didn't know Billie Jean as well as Raelyn did but I knew for damn sure that she would never in a million years sit around knitting.

"You're dreaming, pretty girl."

She rolled her eyes again. The sass was damn strong with her today. "You think we can go inside now so you and your badass friends can save my sister?"

"That's the plan." I pressed a quick kiss to her lips. "And try to keep a cap on the sass," I whispered against her lips. I threaded my fingers through hers and pulled her toward the clubhouse.

"This place looks a hell of a lot different in the sunlight," she muttered.

The clubhouse really wasn't much to look at. A large brick building that didn't reveal what was inside. The row of motorcycles out front hinted about what it was, but other than a small sign with the club's patch next to the door, there wasn't anything else.

"You want a huge light up arrow pointing at the door announcing what it is?" I laughed. "Be glad it's semi clean and doesn't smell like ass."

Raelyn wrinkled her nose. "I suppose you're right. I can only imagine how many guys call this place home."

"About half. Some of the guys have their own places."

"Do you?"

I shook my head and pulled open the door. "Nope. The club is my life. Everything I need is right here."

"Is that so?' she muttered.

"You're here right now so I can say that."

"Smooth," she whispered and patted my chest. "Next you're gonna tell me you were a celibate saint before you met me."

"Uh, well, I would try to lie but the name kind of gives away my past." The door closed behind us. All of the guys were scattered around the common room.

"As long as that stays in your past, I'll be fine."

"That's all in the past, pretty girl."

"Keep it that way."

"Raelyn!"

Great. Leona was still here. How she had managed to get Barracuda in her grasp was beyond me.

She pulled Raelyn away from me and folded her into a huge hug. "I can't believe she actually called you," she yelled.

It was way too early for this. I managed to grab the thermos of coffee from Raelyn and headed to the bar. I was going to need a little bit of something extra in my coffee.

Jet, Monk, and Barracuda sat at the bar each with cups of steaming coffee in front of them.

"You need a little something extra in there?" Monk asked me. He grabbed a bottle of bourbon and set it on the bar.

"Read my mind." I pulled the cork and poured a healthy glug into the thermos. I took a sip and winced. "Now that'll put some hair on your chest."

I leaned against the bar and watched Leona fuss over Raelyn.

"Still can't believe you're bedding her and she doesn't talk your ear off."

Barracuda grunted. "I have my ways of silencing her."

We watched Leona and Raelyn for a couple of minutes before Barracuda bellowed, "Church!"

Hell. Raelyn was not going to be happy. She wasn't going to be able to hear anything.

The guys filed down the hallway, and I lingered behind.

"Playboy," Raelyn whined. "Are you sure you can't sneak me in or something?"

I shook my head. "It's better this way, pretty girl. You don't need to worry about anything. We'll figure out how to get Billie Jean back, and you can just hang out with Leona."

Leona snapped her gum and smiled. "I know where they hide the good booze, babe. Stick with me. It'll be a hell of a lot more fun than stodgy church."

Raelyn wrinkled her nose. "You do know that it's not an actual church, right?"

Leona flitted her hand. "Don't really care what it is. Sounds boring." She flopped down on the couch and grabbed the remote.

"Just hang out here, and I'll be out as soon as I can."

Raelyn huffed, but she didn't protest anymore. She leaned up on her tiptoes and

174

popped a kiss to my lips. "I trust you, Playboy. Just bring my sister home and make sure you come back with her."

I wrapped an arm around her and pulled her close. "I'll always come back to you, pretty girl." I pressed one last kiss against her lips.

"I think you two have to be the record for falling in love," Leona called. "I mean, really. It's like you two have known each other for forever."

Raelyn rolled her eyes and pressed her forehead to mine. "She said she spiked her coffee. It's barely eight o'clock, Playboy. I'm pretty sure by the time your meeting is over, she'll be passed out."

"Well, tell her welcome to the club." I held up my thermos. "So did I and a few of the other guys."

Raelyn grabbed the thermos and shook her head. "That is not the reason why I gave you a huge thermos. This is supposed to keep you energized, not get you drunk off your butt." She raised it to her nose and took a whiff. "Sweet jesus, Playboy. How much did you put in here?"

I held up my fingers two inches apart. "Just a bit."

She pointed to the hallway the guys had walked down. "You can have this back after you figure out how to save my sister."

"Your sass is getting pretty bold," I warned.

She flounced over to the couch and sat next to Leona. "You like it," she called.

She was damn right about that.

I did like it. And I was also going to like trying to work it out of her in the bedroom when this was all over.

The good thing was I knew nothing was going to take away Raelyn's sass, but pretending like I needed to fuck it out of her was going to be fun.

*

Raelyn

Leona and I stared at each other.

"We're both gonna yell at each other, yeah?"

I nodded. "Though I think mine is just more wanting to know what you are doing."

She rolled her eyes. "Having fun? Getting in my kicks when I can get them? Pretty sure we're doing the same thing."

Was I having fun? Yeah. But I was doing a whole hell of a lot more than that.

She eyed me knowingly. "Except you're in it a whole of a lot deeper than I am."

Damn. I hated that Leona knew me so well. Anyone else I could have sat there and agreed that I was having fun with Playboy and not catching feelings for him. Leona knew just by looking at me that I was in it good.

"I don't know what you're talking about."

Leona silenced the TV. She turned toward me and pressed a knee into the couch. "I don't blame you, honey. I can see the way that man looks at you. He's in it for more than fun, too. Hell, he might be into it more than you are at the moment. I peeked out the window and saw him talking to you before you walked in. Treating you like you're a fragile package."

"He's not doing that."

She tipped her head to the side and pursed her lips. "You must be walking around with your eyes shut if you're gonna try to deny that he's looking at you with some major puppy dog eyes."

I wouldn't go that far. "Can we stop talking about this?"

She shook her head.

"I think there are some other things we should be talking about. I think we should focus on Billie Jean." *Anything* other than Playboy and me.

"Barracuda and the Royal Bastards are taking care of Billie Jean. You'd be foolish to sit there and worry she wasn't coming back home. You know she's alive, and there's a room full of badass men who are willing to do anything to get her back."

"But you're not being foolish sitting there telling me there isn't anything happening between Barracuda and you?"

"The way Barracuda looks at me and the way Playboy looks at you is entirely different. I know what Barracuda wants from me, and that's all I want from him."

"So nothing more could happen?"

Leona rolled her eyes. "Quit trying to make Barracuda and me a thing in your head. I'm not saying never, but the odds of it happening are slim to none. We're enjoying each other and then going on our ways when we have enough."

With that attitude, yeah, nothing was going to happen.

"What if you and me talking about Barracuda helps me to not sit here and worry about Billie Jean?"

Leona flipped me off. "You're a bitch."

178

I batted my eyes. "I mean, I haven't thought about Billie Jean since Playboy left. I'm focused on you. If you want me to stop talking about Barracuda and you, I think you're doing a disservice to our friendship."

She grabbed the remote and pointed it at the TV. "How about you can talk about it but that doesn't mean I have to? Or, you can talk about it and I'll build up this whole grand lie about it, yeah?"

She would do that, except I would know everything was a damn lie. I took a sip of Playboy's coffee and cringed. "Oh, my God. It's like he put half the bottle in here."

Leona grabbed the cup and took a sip. "Tastes okay to me."

I held up my hand when she tried to hand it back. "Keep it." I cringed and stuck my tongue out.

She turned back to the TV and tucked both of her legs underneath her. "Suit yourself."

I sat back on the couch and tried to focus on the TV. "Thank you for trying to distract me," I mumbled.

She tipped her glass to me. "That's what best friends do."

*

Chapter Fifteen

Playboy

Another 10k gone…

"Shit with the Kings of Vengeance is set."

"They're opening up a Skinz in Whitmore?" Tank asked.

Barracuda nodded. "We pay the Devil's Rebels the thirty grand they lost when the Kings blew up their clubhouse, charge the Kings interest on the loan, let them use the Skinz name for the new business venture, and then take a skim off the profits."

"We come out good in the end?" Monk asked.

Barracuda nodded. "We come out with about fifteen K on the loan and if they manage the club well, we'll be more than flush in the end. I talked to Nycto from Tampa and Hype in Miami. They both think it's a pretty solid fucking deal for us and the Kings."

"Nycto still a crazy fuck?" Mace asked.

"You know that isn't ever going to change." Barracuda ran a finger around the rim of his cup. "The money was delivered yesterday. The Kings of Vengeance are out from under the Devil's Rebels but now we might be tangling with them with the whole Billie Jean and Memphis situation."

"But why the hell would the Devil's Rebels be involved with Jester?" Monk asked. "None of this shit is making sense."

I sighed. "Billie Jean said she saw one Devil's Rebels cut. Maybe they aren't a major player in any of this. Billie Jean said she got in deep with Jester. He's not a part of the Rebels. Two years ago, he had a run in with them himself. I doubt the Rebels would align with him or patch him in."

"You're probably right." Barracuda drummed his fingers on the table. "So, the question is, do we reach out to the Devil's Rebels or try to avoid them?"

"What do we know?" Tank replied. "Jester and whoever this Mac guy is are the two names we have. Jester is in drugs. He's been dealing for the past fifteen years. Whatever he is doing with Billie Jean and Memphis has to do with that."

Raelyn would hate where we were headed with this, but it was hard to sit and ignore the fact that the person Billie Jean had gotten in trouble with was a known drug dealer.

"Why the hell would those two get involved with him?" I asked.

"Money talks, brother. I'm assuming he was paying them pretty good to do whatever it was." Jinx shook his head. "I know Memphis was going through some shit and was picking up extra shifts at the club. If Jester came around at the right time, I'm sure whatever deal they struck was a good one."

Barracuda raised his voice. "We need to stop speculating and stick to what we know. We find Jester and we'll find Billie Jean and Memphis."

"And how the hell are we going to do that?" Monk asked.

"We use the one card we have. Call the Devil's Rebels, talk to Menace, and let him know about one of his guys hanging with Jester." A smile spread across Barracuda's mouth. "I doubt he'd be very happy to hear that."

Barracuda pulled out his phone and set it on the table. He swiped a few buttons and the phone rang. No one answered, and it went to a recording saying the voicemail had yet to be set up.

Six-Gun groaned. "How the fuck do—"

The phone rang, and Barracuda connected the call and hit the speakerphone button. "You got Barracuda."

"Why the fuck are you calling me again? We got the money."

"Hello, Menace," Barracuda drawled.

"Don't talk to me like we're fucking friends, asshole."

This guy seemed really nice.

"I just had a little bit of information fall into my lap, and I was thinking you might like to hear it." Barracuda's voice was smooth and cocky. We weren't sure this was going to work, but Barracuda had to sell it.

"I'm not interested in whatever it is you're selling," Menace grunted.

"Oh, but I think you might. It has to do with one of your men, Jester, and a guy named Mac."

Menace growled. "My men have nothing to do with Jester, and I don't know who the fuck Mac is."

Barracuda smiled. "Well, I think you might be wrong on that one. I've got a pretty good source telling me they saw one of your cuts at Jester's place."

"Since when do you have info that involves Jester? You and I may not like each other, but we both agree Jester is a fucking cancer we don't want to be involved with."

Barracuda sighed. "Well, that may be true, but Jester has a couple things that belong to us and we're trying to get them back. Problem is, we don't know where he is."

"So you want to talk to my guy that was with him," Menace sussed out.

"You got it."

"What the hell do I get out of it besides kicking the shit out of the guy?"

"Name your price," Barracuda offered.

"Another ten grand should be enough."

The Devil's Rebels were always looking for more money. Well, that and women to sell. Thank God they hadn't wanted anything like that. The Sacramento chapter of the Royal Bastards was into selling the legal kind of sex.

"I'll have it for you as soon as you give me the location on Jester."

"And I'm just supposed to take your word on it?"

Barracuda leaned forward and spoke clearly. "Have I ever fucked with you, Menace? Give me the location and the money is yours."

Menace grunted. "Fine. I'll have it for you within the hour. I've got two guys who have a blow problem. It was probably one of those assholes trying to score off Jester. I give you the location of Jester and I have the money in my account within fifteen minutes. For every minute you're late, add a grand." The call disconnected.

"And just like that, we'll have the location of Jester." Barracuda grabbed the phone. "I'm assuming you'll be willing to put up half of the ten?" he asked me.

I nodded. I had a pretty hefty stash of money, and I was more than willing to use some of it to get Billie Jean back. I would do it for Raelyn.

"The club will put up the other five. Depending on what the hell Memphis did, we'll get it from her in the end." Barracuda leaned back in his chair. "The Devil's Rebels got forty grand of my money within two days. What the fuck is this world coming to?"

"At least you'll get most of it paid back with interest," Jinx pointed out.

"I'd much rather have the money stay with us then having to bail people out," Barracuda growled.

Five minutes later, the phone rang with the information we needed.

Menace cut straight to the point. "Dumbass Carpenter was the one hanging out with Jester. I'm assuming you're after the two girls he saw in the basement."

"You'd be correct," Barracuda drawled.

"He said the blonde was pretty beat up and being used as a fuck doll. The other one was beat up, but he didn't think they were touching her."

"So where are they?" Barracuda asked. We would worry about what happened to them after we got them back.

"Elk Grove. House on the edge of town." Menace rattled off the address. "Now get me my money." The line went dead.

Barracuda looked to Monk.

"I'm on it," Monk mumbled. He grabbed his laptop and set it on the table. "I was hoping we were going to make the asshole wait for a second, but I'll just get him paid right away."

Two minutes later, ten grand was in Menace's account and we had the information we needed to get Billie Jean and Memphis back.

"All right," Barracuda drawled. "Let's go."

*

Chapter Sixteen

Raelyn

You can't just leave me...

"That was quick," Leona whispered.

The guys walked straight from church and right out the front door.

Playboy was one of the last ones. He headed to me and pulled me up from the couch.

"What's happening?" I demanded.

"We're gonna go get Billie Jean and Memphis, pretty girl."

"You know where she is?" I cried.

Playboy nodded. "We know where she is, and we're gonna bring her home."

"Oh, my God," I gasped. I had never heard sweeter words. Billie Jean was going to come home. "Where is she? Why did they take her?"

Playboy shook his head. "I told you not to worry. You don't need to know any of that."

"I'm going with you, Playboy. I'm going with you to get her," I insisted.

He frowned and grimaced. "No, you're not. I can't risk bringing you with us and then something happening to you."

"I can't sit here and just twiddle my thumbs waiting for you to come back," I pleaded. "I *have* to come with you."

He glanced over his shoulder. Two guys I had never talked to before stood there. "Jinx is going to stay with you and Leona while we're gone."

I shook my head. "No," I yelled.

"I'm not going to stand here and argue with you about this, Raelyn."

"But why can't I come?! She's my sister!" The hysterics kicked in. This is what I had been waiting for, and now, I couldn't help bring her home. "You can't do this!"

"Raelyn." Barracuda's voice boomed through the common room. "Calm your shit down or no one is leaving."

What did that mean? He wouldn't go get Billie Jean? He couldn't do that.

"Just let me come with." I was beyond desperate to finally see my sister.

"Keep your ass here. We've already got enough trouble going on. We don't need to add in your hysterical ass." Barracuda folded his arms over his chest. "You come along and Playboy is going to be distracted by you. Stay. Here."

I didn't want to distract Playboy. I didn't want to distract any of them. I just wanted my sister back. "Just…" I closed my eyes and tried to calm my racing heart. I opened my eyes and looked up at Playboy. "Just bring her home."

*

Chapter Seventeen

Playboy

Night night, fucker…

"Tank said he's only picking up four people upstairs. Looks like two are sleeping and the other two are by the front door."

"Any clue on the girls?" Barracuda asked.

I shook my head. "He can't pick anything up in the basement."

"So either they're dead and cold or that thermal shit can't reach the basement," Jet stated.

That was what I was hoping. I promised Raelyn I would bring her sister home. I didn't want to do that with a body bag.

"We're ready in the back," Tank's voice cackled over the radio.

We were going with the element of surprise. Jester was never going to see us coming.

Jet, Barracuda, and I walked down the alleyway next to the house that Jester and his dumbasses were in.

"We really just gonna knock on the door?" Jet asked.

Barracuda shrugged. "Why the hell not? I doubt Jester would expect that."

"I doubt he would have expected a fucking grenade launcher either," Jet muttered.

"Because launching a grenade into the place won't kill everyone inside," I drawled. I was all for destroying Jester, but I didn't want to kill Billie Jean and Memphis in the process.

We walked to the front porch, and Barracuda pounded on the door.

"We can't even bust the door down?" Jet grumbled.

"How about you cool your fucking jets, huh?" I suggested.

Jet flipped me off. "Like I haven't heard that before."

Barracuda banged on the door again.

It swung open, and Jester stood there.

Well, that wasn't hard to get him.

"Hey, Jester," Barracuda drawled. "Long time, no talk. You mind if we come in for a second?"

He scrambled to shut the door, but Jet managed to wedge his foot inside. "You're not gonna invite us in?" Jet laughed.

Jester screamed and tried to take off back into the house.

I grabbed him around the neck and pushed him down onto his knees. "Where do you think you're going?" I sneered.

Barracuda and Jet walked in, and I pulled Jester onto his feet. "We just wanna talk to you, Jester. Why are you trying to run?"

I slammed the door shut behind me and moved into the place.

There wasn't much in here.

A large TV leaned against a wall, and there were a couple couches scattered around. "You should really try to do a little something with the place," I muttered. "Take some pride in where you live."

"If ya get high enough, you can just imagine nice shit in here," Jet laughed.

A guy jumped out from behind the couch and tried to hit Barracuda. Barracuda managed to easily step to the side and avoid the punch.

Barracuda grabbed him by the arm, twisted it behind his back and pushed him to the floor. "Better luck next time," he grunted.

"Got the other two!" Tank, Monk, and Mace appeared from the back and were dragging two guys with them.

"I really doubted we would get a jump in these guys with just knocking on the door, but obviously it worked," Tank laughed.

Monk and Mace threw the two guys toward Jester, and they fell in a heap.

It had been a couple of years since I had actually seen Jester. The drugs were not doing him any favors. He may have had a lot of money, but he had gotten into sampling his product a little too much.

His eyes were sunken with dark circles around them, and he was a bag of bones. It was amazing he was able to stand up. A slight breeze probably could have knocked him over.

I pushed him on the floor and reached for my gun. I pointed it at his head and smiled. "Run. I dare ya."

I wanted nothing more than to shoot this fucker right in the face. I hated him long before he had decided to kidnap Billie Jean and Memphis.

Barracuda sat on the couch in front of the four guys. Tank, Monk, and Mace stood off to the sides, and I waited behind the couch. Jet stayed next to the pile of dumbasses.

"We don't want any fucking trouble," Jester drawled. "I don't know what you're even doing here."

"If you don't want any trouble, then why the hell are you kidnapping women?" Mace asked. "Pretty sure that falls under the definition of trouble."

"I don't know what you're talking about," Jester snapped.

Barracuda stood up and shrugged. "Well crap, guys, he doesn't know what we're talking about. We must have the wrong drug dealer."

Monk moved and stood over the guy who had tried to take a swing at Barracuda. "Mac?" he asked.

The guy shook his head vehemently. "I, uh, I don't know no Mac."

Monk shook his head. "Well, you sure the fuck look like him."

"He's the guy from the club?" Barracuda asked.

"Sure the fuck looks like him. If he's not Mac, then he's got a fucking twin walking around." Monk reached down and grabbed the guy by his hair. He lifted him up and turned him to Barracuda.

"Yeah. Looks just like the guy who took Billie Jean and Memphis," Barracuda agreed. He nodded to Mace and Tank. "Go find the girls," he ordered. He sat down and leaned back into the couch. "Which one of you is going to tell me what the hell is going on? Possibly be able to walk out of here without a bullet inside of you?" Barracuda drawled.

No one spoke. The three cowered on the ground, and Jester just stared at Barracuda.

Barracuda pulled his gun from the waist of his pants and pointed at one of the guys Mace and Tank and brought in. "Well, I'll just start shooting until one of you starts talking." He fired a shot and hit the guy in the arm.

"Ow." I cringed. "Not gonna kill you, but it's gonna leave a fucking mark," I muttered.

The guy clutched his arm and screamed. He wailed in pain and flailed around on the ground.

"Anyone have something to say?" Barracuda asked again.

I had to give it to these guys. They were keeping their mouths shut. One of their friends had just gotten shot and no one spoke.

"Maybe they need a little bit more motivation to talk," I mumbled to Barracuda.

"You may be right." He centered his gun over the other guy Monk and Mace had brought in. "Leg or arm?" he asked politely.

The guy tried to scramble away but ran into Jet.

Jet looked at the asshole. "These guys are fucking morons. How in the hell did they manage to get the drop on Memphis and Billie Jean?"

Barracuda shot him in the leg with no warning. "Anyone want to talk now?"

"Stop!" Mac shouted.

Barracuda glanced at me over his shoulder. "My money was on this guy. He doesn't seem like the type who can take a shot."

Jet lifted him up and moved him toward Barracuda. "Speak, fucker."

The guy licked his dry lips.

"You fucking talk and you're dead," Jester growled.

Barracuda pointed his gun at Jester's head. "As if you're in the position to threaten killing someone."

"Spoiler," Jet laughed. "You're all gonna die."

"Not so fast," Barracuda said. "I did say if one of them talked, they may walk out of here with no extra holes in them." He nodded to Mac. "Start talking."

"The girls. They were running some of the drugs for us. The blonde was the one who started. She needed money and was willing to do anything." The guy licked his lips again. "The one with the ever changing hair color is the one who stirred shit up."

"Shut your mouth!" Jester spat.

I pointed my gun at Jester. "You tell him to shut up one more time and I'm gonna put a bullet between your eyes."

"We needed one more girl to help and the blonde suggested her friend," Mac continued. "Things were going good until we started noticing some of the drugs came up missing. Not a lot, but enough for us to know something wasn't right."

"The girls you were using were stealing from you?" Monk asked.

"We didn't know what was happening. We didn't figure it out until last week."

Jet smacked him upside the head. "Well tell us what the fuck happened, dumbass."

"She's a snitch. An informant for the cops."

Whoa.

"The girls?" Barracuda asked.

"Just the one. The blonde had no idea what Billie Jean was doing."

Raelyn had been right. There was no way she was doing drugs. She was snitching to the cops about Jester.

"So why take both girls?" I asked.

"Because at the time, we didn't know which one of them was ratting to the cops. All we noticed was the white car parked in different spots but there every day. They were surveilling us and using the information Billie Jean had given them."

"She was skimming off the drugs to give to the cops as evidence," Monk snickered. "Fucking smart."

"She's a fucking rat," Jester spat. "Nothing smart about that. I should have killed that bitch right away when we grabbed her. The couple grand I was going to get for her and Memphis is the only reason they're still alive."

"But, ya didn't." Mace drawled.

Tank and Mace walked in with Billie Jean and Memphis. Their clothes were ripped and dirty, and they both looked like they had gone ten rounds in the ring.

"Had to break down the door to the basement. They were right on the other side of it," Tank informed us.

They were alive, but they looked rough. Memphis' left eye was swollen shut, and she wasn't wearing pants. She had bruises all over her face and a large gash on her arm.

Billie Jean's hair was matted down with dried blood, and her lip was swollen and bleeding. She had all of her clothes on, but they were ripped and filthy.

Menace had told us they were raping Memphis.

Anger boiled deep inside me. Who the fuck did Jester think he was to do this? Where the fuck did he get off?

I pointed the gun at Jester's head and slowly moved around the couch.

"Playboy," Barracuda called.

I didn't stop. I couldn't.

I pressed the end of the gun against Jester's forehead. "You think you're a big man? Raping women and beating them? That makes you feel strong?"

"She...she's a snitch, and we only touched the blonde. Fucking Billie Jean doesn't do anything for me," Jester stuttered. A rapist with disconerning taste.

As if that made what he had done right. "You're a fucking coward. Use women to haul your drugs around while you sit here in your fucking roach infested filth getting high every day." There was a special place in hell for guys like Jester.

I never would tell you I was one of the good guys, but I had some morals. Raping and beating women was lower than dirt.

"Take the girls out to the van," Barracuda ordered Mace and Tank.

Mace wrapped his arm around Memphis' shoulder, and she whimpered when he urged her to walk. He lifted her into his arms, careful not to jostle her, and carried her out the door.

Tank put his arm around Billie Jean and tried to follow Mace.

"Wait," Billie Jean said.

She hobbled over to Jester and looked down at him.

"What do you have to say, snitch?" he spat. Even with a gun to his head, Jester was a fucking moron.

I ground the barrel into his skin, and my finger itched to pull the trigger.

"Burn in hell, you piece of shit." Billie Jean growled and spit on him. "You deserve everything they're gonna do to you." Billie Jean had the same spunk as Raelyn.

Tank led her out of the house, and the door slammed shut behind them.

"Not how you saw this ending, did you, Jester?" Barracuda moved next to me and looked down at Jester. "You've always thought you were untouchable."

"Not anymore," Jet called.

"I'm just like you guys. You think you're better than me, but you're the fucking same," Jester growled. Even in the eye of death, he was a mouthy fucker.

The two Barracuda had shot whimpered on the floor in pain and pleaded for their lives.

Jet crouched down and pushed the tip of his gun into the wound in the one's arm. "That hurt?" he asked.

The guy moaned and tried to move from Jet.

Jet pinned him to the floor with his knee. "Can I kill this one first?" he asked.

"They're all going to die," Barracuda replied. "Don't give a fuck in what order."

"You said I would live!" Mac yelled.

Barracuda pinned him with a glare. "No. I said you *might* live."

"You can't do this!" Mac wailed.

Barracuda walked over to him and kicked him in the gut. He pointed his gun at him and planted a foot in his chest to pin him to the floor. "No one tells me what to do." He pulled the trigger and shot Mac right between the eyes. Blood spattered all over the floor, and Mac's eyes rolled into the back of his head.

Jet followed Barracuda's lead and pressed the gun to the one with the arm wound. "Night night, fucker." He pulled the trigger and watched the life drain from the guy.

The one with the leg wound tried to run away but collapsed onto the floor in a heap. Jet spun, fired twice, and killed him.

"What the hell, man?" Monk grumbled. "I didn't get to shoot one."

"Gotta be quicker than that," Jet shrugged.

"And then there was one," I growled.

"Please, no," Jester pleaded. "Maybe we can work something out. We could work together."

Barracuda barked with laughter. "You think you could work with the Royal Bastards?"

"Snort some more, Jester," Jet laughed.

"No! You guys could branch out. I could give you all of my contacts an—"

I didn't want to hear anymore. Nothing was going to stop me from putting a bullet in his head.

I pulled the trigger, and his head exploded. "Times up, fucker." His body collapsed at my feet with a thud.

"Jesus," Jet muttered. "You splattered his fucking brains on my boots. Do brains wash out?" He shook his foot, and the spongy tissue fell on the floor.

"Are we cleaning this up?" I asked

Barracuda shook his head. "Leave them like this. The police can send a thank you card for taking out the fucking trash."

A gurgling noise came from the guy who had tried to run. "Damn. This one has got some fight in him," Jet muttered. He put four more bullets in him, and he stopped making noise.

"I think it was just the hot air leaving his body," I laughed.

"Well, God knows these assholes were full of it."

I tucked my gun in the waistband of my pants and followed Barracuda out the front door.

"The girls are all loaded up. There was a blanket in the trunk we gave it to Memphis," Tank said.

"They say anything?" Barracuda asked.

Mace shook his head. "Billie Jean was taking care of Memphis. I think she's pretty banged up."

Barracuda nodded to Tank. "Take them to the clubhouse. We'll call the doc and have him come out."

Tank and Mace hopped into the car and headed to the clubhouse.

"You believe that shit?" Monk asked.

"What? That Billie Jean was an informant?" Barracuda asked.

Monk nodded.

"I can believe it. The chick shoots straight from the hip," Barracuda laughed. He shook his head. "She's got a lot of spunk in her, too. Spit on his dumbass and told him to go to hell."

Jet tucked his gun in his waistband. "Well, now that that's over, can we get the hell out of here?"

"Yeah, brother." Barracuda looked back at the house with four dead bodies in it. "I think we did pretty good and it's not even noon yet."

It was over. Billie Jean and Memphis were safe.

Raelyn had her sister back. She was a little more battered than the last time Raelyn had seen her, but she was safe again.

I threw my leg over my bike and cranked it up.

Jester was dead.

Billie Jean was back home.

Now it was time to really make Raelyn mine.

*

Chapter Eighteen

Raelyn

Say what?!

"Stop staring at me."

I couldn't. I didn't know if I would ever see Billie Jean again and now she was sitting in front of me. "I can't."

She rolled her eyes and grabbed her glass off the bar. "You keep staring, I'm going home."

I looked away for a second but then my eyes were back on her. "You're not leaving."

She shook her head. "I'm gonna leave eventually, Raelyn. I have my own place and life to get back to."

"I know, Billie. Can I just have one night where you're right in front of me?" Jesus. She was acting like she hadn't just been kidnapped for over a week.

I had been watching out the window the whole time Playboy was gone. The van pulled into the driveway, and my heart leapt when the passenger door opened and Billie Jean had stepped out.

"I'm not staying," she stated quietly.

"I know, Billie Jean," I growled. She was going to give me one damn night.

"No, Raelyn. I'm not just talking about tonight. I mean I'm not staying here. I can't stay in Sacramento anymore." She looked down at her hands. "Before the whole Jester thing, I didn't know what I wanted to do with my life, but I knew I didn't want to be here anymore."

"But..." I trailed off. I didn't know what to say. Billie Jean was my sister, and we always lived in the same city. Yes, she had her own life, but she was always just a phone call or short drive away.

"I became an informant for the SPD and something changed inside me, Raelyn. I found something that could make a difference. I was doing something worthwhile. Not slinging drinks at some strip club and wasting my life away." She sighed and ran her finger around the rim of her glass. "I applied to become a police officer in Colorado Springs. My testing starts next week."

I blinked slowly and tried to process what Billie Jean had just said. "Is there Colorado Springs in California that I don't know about?"

Billie Jean laughed and shook her head. "No, Raelyn. I meant it when I said I can't stay here. I have to get out of California."

"But, you're my sister." I had just got Billie Jean back, and now, she was going to leave me again?

"And I'll still be your sister, Raelyn. Just from Colorado."

I looked down at my empty cup. "I can't drive to Colorado when I'm bored or want to go shopping with you."

"Yeah, I think the over eighteen hour drive might be a bit too much for one day," Billie Jean laughed. She sounded happy. I hadn't heard her sound like that for a while. She was genuinely happy.

"You're all I have, Billie Jean. If you leave, I'll be all alone." I couldn't get over my own feelings though.

Billie Jean shook her head. "I'm not all you have, Raelyn." She turned and looked over her shoulder. "You have crazy Leona."

Leona was sitting in Barracuda's lap with a beer in her hand and a huge smile on her face.

Billie Jean looked back at me. "And you also have Playboy now."

"Why didn't you ever tell me you weren't happy?" I wasn't ready to get off the topic of Billie Jean leaving. I knew she was trying to distract me from the fact that my only sister was going to another state.

She sighed. "It's not that I wasn't happy, I just knew that there was something more for me out there. I'm meant to be more than a waitress for the rest of my life."

I agreed, but did she have to leave the damn state? "You're putting two states in between us." I leaned forward. "And they're not small states like Connecticut or Maryland." Nevada and Utah were huge in comparison. She herself had just said it was an over eighteen hour drive.

"No, they're not, but it's just a short airplane ride away, Raelyn. I have to do this. I know it's going to be a big change, but I finally figured out what I want to do with my life."

I sighed. I was being selfish and not thinking about what Billie Jean wanted. "What about Vegas?" I asked. That was still over an eight-hour drive, but it was closer than freaking Colorado Springs.

"I've made up my mind, Raelyn. I already bought my plane ticket."

"You were just kidnapped for over a week, Billie Jean. Don't you think you should rest for a little bit?" She could wait. Put her plans on hold until she was fully healed. Hell, it was June. She might as well as give it six months and try again next year.

"Oh, Raelyn. You always are the best big sister, even if you were only seven minutes older. I know you're just worried about me going off and you not being right there with me, but I need to go." She laid her hand on mine. "You're gonna be fine without me. You're finally starting your life here. Never in a million years would I have put you and Playboy together, but it makes sense. You're exactly what he needs to grow up, and he's exactly what you need to spice up life a little bit."

"We're not talking about me."

Billie Jean grabbed her glass and stood up. "We should, Raelyn. We're always talking about me and never about you."

"That's because…" I didn't know why. "I've got everything figured out. I live a boring life, and it's always going to be that way."

Billie Jean shook her head. "And now I'm getting everything figured out."

"But you never told me you wanted to be a police officer."

She shrugged. "Because I didn't know I wanted to do it until a couple of months ago." She put her arm around my shoulders and pressed a kiss to my face. "You've been a great big sister, Raelyn, and I'll always be thankful for all of your sacrifices. It's time for me to set out on my own and let you live your life now."

"Billie Jean, I—"

"I'm gonna go check on Memphis and call it a night. I'll see you in the morning." She gave me one last squeeze and headed down the hall to Memphis.

"Pretty girl." Playboy took Billie Jean's seat and frowned. "I caught the tail end of that. You okay?"

I blinked back tears and tried to smile. "Never better." I kept telling myself after we brought Billie Jean home that everything would go back to normal.

Billie Jean living in Colorado Springs was not normal.

"You're a horrible liar." He grabbed my hand and pressed a kiss to my palm.

Adding Playboy to my life was the only new change I wanted. Billie Jean leaving was not okay.

A tear streaked down my cheek. "Billie Jean is leaving for Colorado Springs next week to join the police academy."

Playboy's jaw dropped. "That was the last thing I expected you to say."

I felt the same when she had told me. "Billie Jean can't be a cop, Playboy."

He tipped his head to the side. "Why not?"

"Uh, well…she…" I sputtered.
"Because she can't."

"I hope that wasn't the reasoning you gave her."

I growled and drained my glass of whiskey. "No. I told her she couldn't go because I needed her here in California. It's ridiculous to move to Colorado when there are plenty of police stations she can work at here."

"But maybe she doesn't want to be here, pretty girl. And what do you *need* her for? You want her here."

"Whose side are you on?" I snapped.

Playboy chuckled. "Always yours, Raelyn. I think you just need to take a second to think and not just feel."

"My sister was kidnapped for over a week, Playboy, and now, she thinks she's just going to hop on a plane and fly to Colorado."

"But she can, Raelyn. Maybe that's what *she* needs," he tried to reason.

"And what I feel doesn't matter?" I screeched. Billie Jean was back home, and I was still on my crazy emotional roller coaster.

Playboy tried to gather me in his arms, but I pushed away.

He sighed heavily. "Of course what you feel matters, Raelyn, but Billie Jean is living her life. She's a big girl and can decide if she wants to move away."

"And just what am I supposed to do if she leaves? She's all I've ever had."

Playboy grabbed my hand and threaded his fingers through mine. "You've got me now, pretty girl. You've got your own life to live."

I stared at his hand and felt his warmth seep into my skin. "She's always been there," I whispered. "She's my sister, and I'm supposed to protect her. I can't do that two states away."

Playboy reached for me, and this time, I didn't resist. He lifted me into his lap and wrapped his arms around me. "She'll still be your little sister, and you can still protect her."

"Yeah," I whined, "from a million miles away."

"I think it's more like twelve hundred miles, pretty girl."

"Same difference," I mumbled.

He nuzzled my cheek. "Just think of the vacations we can take to visit her. Colorado is pretty beautiful during the winter. We can visit your sister and make a run up to Breckenridge for skiing while we're there."

"We, huh?" I giggled. Maybe snowy vacations with Playboy didn't sound too bad. We barely ever got snow in Sacramento, and the idea of cuddling up by a fireplace with Playboy sounded pretty inviting.

"I want there to be a *we*, Raelyn. I know we've barely spent much time together in the grand scheme of things, but we've got forever to spend with each other, if you want."

I tipped my head back and looked up at him. "Is the playboy giving up the game?" I laughed.

He shrugged. "I never really liked the game. I was just bored and playing until you showed up."

"Is that so?" I laughed. "I think I just heard hearts all over Sacramento break."

He delved his fingers into my hair and leaned close. "There's only one heart I care about."

"Hmm," I hummed. "Such sweet words. Do you use them on all of the girls?"

"Just you, pretty girl. You're all I see anymore."

"But I'm nothing like those girls you used to date."

He pressed a kiss to my lips. "Two things. I didn't date."

I rolled my eyes.

"And the reason I like you is because you *aren't* those girls."

That got an even bigger eye roll. "You're over the sexy and beautiful type?"

"Have I ever told you you've got some major attitude?"

"You might have mentioned sass a time or two."

He gave me another kiss. "So, are you ready for your new normal?"

I pressed my forehead to his. "My sister moving far away? No. Not ready. But you? Yeah, I'm ready for you to be my new normal."

"It sure is going to be an interesting ride, pretty girl."

I sighed and kissed him. "I'm ready."

*

Chapter Nineteen

Playboy

Who knows?

"Is she going to be okay?"

Barracuda shrugged. "The doc said she'll heal."

Six-Gun lowered his voice. "You know what I'm asking."

"I don't think anyone is going to know the answer to that besides Memphis." Monk sat back in his chair and folded his arms over his chest. "I sure as hell wish I could go back and kill that fucker Jester again."

We all felt that way. Killing him a hundred times wouldn't be enough justice for what he had done to Memphis.

A week had passed since we killed Jester and his fucked up crew, but my blood still boiled at the thought of what he had done to Memphis and Billie Jean.

Yesterday, Raelyn and I drove Billie Jean to the airport to start her new life. The whole way there, Raelyn had tried to convince her to stay and be a police officer in Sacramento. Finally, Billie Jean had blown up at her and said she couldn't live there anymore.

She couldn't live in the city that had almost destroyed her. Billie Jean was going through some emotional shit, and the only way she was going to get over it was to leave the place it had happened. Raelyn finally gave up trying to convince her to stay and decided to take on the supportive sister role. At least that was until Billie Jean was through security and Raelyn broke down.

She sobbed uncontrollably the whole way home, and she finally cried herself to sleep mumbling about roller coasters and wanting off the damn thing.

Billie Jean was going to be okay. I knew it was going to be hard, but she was tough.

Memphis, on the other hand, had the whole club worried.

"She doesn't want to come out of her room. All she does is sleep." Six-Gun sighed. "I have to force her to eat every day."

Six-Gun had taken it upon himself to personally take care of Memphis. Raelyn had tried to step in, but he had told her he could handle it.

"We'll take it one day at a time with her. No one knows what she went through besides her." Barracuda sighed heavily.

Raelyn had talked to Billie Jean to see if she knew anything, but she didn't. While Jester stuck to beating the hell out of Billie Jean because he hated her for being a rat, he always took Memphis upstairs. Billie Jean said she could hear her scream and cry the whole time, but she couldn't say exactly what happened to her.

"Give her space but keep close," Monk suggested. "If and when she needs something, we'll be there for her."

The Royal Bastards were just that, bastards, but when it came down to it, we all had basic morals.

Hurt only those who deserve it.

Protect those who can't protect themselves.

Memphis was under the protection of the Royal Bastards, and nothing was ever going to touch her again.

*

Chapter Twenty

Raelyn

Leona!

"You were right?"

"Huh?" I asked Leona. It was Saturday afternoon, and Leona and I had pulled two chairs out into the parking lot of the clubhouse and were trying to get some sun. I had knocked on Memphis's door to see if she wanted to come out too, but she hadn't answered.

Leona and I were trying to be there for her but also give her space. I couldn't imagine what she had been through and what she was feeling and thinking now.

Before Billie Jean left yesterday, I had asked her for advice because I knew she was going through sort of the same thing and she had told me to just listen to Memphis. Be there when she wanted us and let her be alone when she needed it.

It was going to be a long road for Memphis, but I believed she would be okay if she let me and Leona in.

"You were right about Barracuda."

"Remind me what I was right about?" I laughed.

Leona reached over and smacked my arm. "About it being more than just fun."

Oh. That. "Are you thinking of keeping a biker dude of your own?"

She glanced at me. "It seems to be working well for you so far."

It was. When I sat back and actually thought about it, it was crazy that Playboy and I had only known each other for a little over two weeks. It felt like a lifetime.

The good thing about meeting someone and instantly falling for them was you still had a lifetime to spend with them. Also jam packing your short time together with a lot of craziness and ups and downs made you get to know each other pretty damn fast.

"I plan on keeping mine."

Leona laughed. "Well, make sure you keep the receipt. I'm sure there's free returns before ninety days."

"You're crazy, Leona," I laughed.

"That's why you need to keep me around, doll. I keep things interesting." She winked and pulled her sunglasses over her eyes. "Now I need to convince Barracuda to keep me around."

"Well, I think you're doing a good job so far."

"Raelyn!"

I turned at Playboy's voice.

"Done with your biker meeting?" I called.

"What are you do—"

A loud engine roared down the road, and I couldn't hear him.

I stood up to walk over to him, and gunfire exploded all around me. I dropped to the ground and covered my head with my arms. "Leona!" I shouted.

I heard a scream rip from her lips, but I couldn't see her.

The gunfire stopped, and the world was silent. My ears rang, and my eyes stung from dust when I fell to the gravel.

"Raelyn!" The world shifted beneath me, and then, I was in Playboy's arms. His hand ran over me frantically , and I tried to see him through the haze.

"Leona," I sputtered. "Where is Leona?" I knocked his hands away and tried to twist around to where Leona had been.

Barracuda barreled past us, and he fell to his knees. "Call an ambulance!" he shouted.

"Let me go!" I screamed at Playboy. "Let me go!"

His arms tightened around me, and he didn't let me down. He moved in the direction of the clubhouse and away from Leona.

I struggled and fought to get out of his arms. "Put me the fuck down!" I twisted in his arms and couldn't see Leona. Monk and Mace rushed by us and hit the ground next to Barracuda.

"Get her in the clubhouse!" Someone shouted.

I heard Monk shout into his phone that they needed an ambulance, and then, Playboy stepped into the clubhouse.

"We can't leave her out there!" I shouted at Playboy.

"She's not alone," Playboy reasoned.

He set me on the couch, and I catapulted up. "What the hell are we doing in here?" I yelled.

Playboy caught me around the waist and held me tight. "Just stay the hell in here, Raelyn. It's not safe out there."

"And that's why we need to get Leona the hell in here!" I got that Playboy was worried about me and wanted to make sure I was safe, but he needed to do the same for Leona.

Mace ran into the clubhouse. His shirt was covered in blood and so were his hands.

"What?' I gasped.

"Shh," Playboy whispered. "Just stay in here, Rae."

My world tilted when Mace ran back outside with a huge first-aid kit. There was so much blood that he left a handprint on the door and there were droplets on the floor.

"Leona," I wailed. I fought against Playboy's hold. "Let me go!" I scratched his arms and managed to break free. I darted out the front door, my hand touching the blood Mace had left there.

"Raelyn!" Playboy called after me.

I had to get to Leona. I had to make sure she was okay. She was my best friend. She was my *only* friend.

My sandal caught on the frame of the door, and I fell. The gravel cut into my bare knees, but I didn't feel it.

Leona.

I had to get to Leona.

I shot up and burst through the crowd around Leona.

Barracuda had his shirt off and was holding it to Leona's chest. The shirt was soaked with blood, and his knuckles were white from gripping the shirt so tightly.

Mace threw open the first aid kit, but I didn't know why.

Leona's eyes were open and lifeless. Barracuda was putting pressure on a bullet wound, but there were at least four other ones on her body oozing blood.

I dropped next to her and put a hand to her cheek. "You can't leave me, Leona. I need to keep you around, remember? We were gonna each have a biker dude." Tears clouded my vision, and a sob escaped my lips. "You can't leave me," I wailed.

Sirens sounded in the distance, and arms circled around my waist. Playboy's familiar touch was there. His touch was the only thing grounding me to the Earth.

Leona laid lifeless in the gravel as the ambulance pulled up and two paramedics jumped out.

Barracuda lifted her limp body into his arms and carried her to the back of the ambulance.

He jumped into the ambulance with her and laid her on the stretcher. A paramedic hopped in back with her and the other rushed back to the driver's seat.

They took off in a whirl of sirens and dust.

Playboy pressed a kiss to the side of my head. "It's okay, Raelyn."

A blood curdling scream ripped from my lips, and I fell to the ground.

Leona was gone.

Chapter Twenty-One

Raelyn

The new normal…

"I brought you purple flowers."

The wind whipped around me.

"You love purple." I dropped to my knees and closed my eyes. "I bet you would have had purple flowers at your wedding and made me wear an obnoxious violet dress."

She didn't answer. She didn't tell me I would have worn whatever she told me to.

"You weren't supposed to leave me, Leona. You and I were supposed to live my new normal together."

One month ago, Leona had died in the parking lot of the Royal Bastards' clubhouse.

The doctor had said she was gone before Barracuda had loaded her into the ambulance. Five gunshots to the chest would do that to a person.

I opened my eyes and wiped the tears from my cheeks.

"Barracuda still isn't back. Monk has been acting as president." I sighed. "So many things changed, but I guess that makes things the new normal right?"

Every week, I had been coming to the cemetery to tell Leona what was happening. She was dead, but she was still my best friend. I told the wind my thoughts and let them ride on the breeze up to her.

Playboy told me when Barracuda found out Leona had died, he went crazy at the hospital. He smashed a window in the waiting area and took off on foot. He made it back to the clubhouse, packed a bag, and took off.

No one had heard from him since.

I sighed and glanced over my shoulder. Playboy stood there like he always did. He waited for me. No matter how long it took, he waited.

"I love him, Leona," I whispered. "He's helping me heal. He's so much more than I thought he was. He makes me happy when all I want to do is cry." The days had passed slowly, but each day, I cried a little less and I loved Playboy a little more.

"I wish you were here to see it, but I know you're watching." I looked back at the large stone with Leona's name scrawled on it. "I better go, Leona. I'll always miss you." I touched the stone and closed my eyes. "Keep an eye on Barracuda. I think he needs it more than I do."

I stood up and brushed off my knees. I walked back to Playboy and wiped my eyes with the back of my hand.

He reached out when I was close and wrapped me in my arms. "Good talk?" he asked.

I tipped my head back and smiled. "Yeah. She was always a good listener."

"Ready to go?"

I nodded. "As long as you're with me."

This was my new normal.

It was a heartbreaking ride. I had lost one of the most important people in my life, but the roller coaster kept going. And as long as Playboy was right next to me, I knew we would make it.

Life was about the ups and the downs and who stuck by you through it all.

Playboy and I were stuck with each other, and I wouldn't want it any other way.

*

Need more?

Six-Gun
Royal Bastards MC: Sacramento
Book 2
coming December 22nd.

Coming Soon

Passing the Torch
Devil's Knights 2nd Generation, Book 1
May 29th

Midnight Wreckage
Kings of Vengeance MC, Book 4
July 29th

About the Author

Winter Travers is a devoted wife, mother, and aunt turned author who was born and raised in Wisconsin. After a brief stint in South Carolina following her heart to chase the man who is now her hubby, they retreated back up North to the changing seasons, and to the place they now call home.

Winter spends her days writing happily ever afters, and her nights being a karate mom hauling her kid to practices and tournaments. She also has an addiction to anything MC related, her puppies, and Mexican food! (Tamales!)

Winter loves to stay connected with her readers. Don't hesitate to reach out and contact her.

Facebook
Twitter
Instagram
Website
Mailing List
Goodreads
BookBub

Have you met the Devil's Knights?

Loving Lo
Devil's Knights Series
Book 1

Chapter 1
Meg

How did just stopping quickly to get dog food and shampoo turn into an overflowing basket and a surplus pack of paper towels?

"Put the paper towels down and back away slowly," I mumbled to myself as I walked past a display of air fresheners and wondered if I needed any.

"Oh dear. Oh, my. I ... Ah ... Oh, my."

I tore my thoughts away from air fresheners and looked down the aisle to an elderly woman who was leaning against the shelf, fanning herself. "Are you ok, ma'am?"

"Oh dear. I just ... I just got a little ... dizzy. " I looked at the woman and saw her hands shaking as she brushed her white hair out of her face. The woman had on denim capris and a white button down short sleeve shirt and surprisingly three-inch wedge heels.

"Ok, well, why don't we try to find you a place to sit down until you get your bearings?" I shifted the basket and paper towels under one arm to help her to the bench that I had seen by the shoe rack two aisles over. "Are you here with anyone?" I asked as I guided her down the aisle.

"Oh no. I'm here by myself. I just needed a few things."

"I only needed two things, and now my basket is overflowing, and I still haven't gotten the things I came in for."

The woman plopped down on the bench chuckling, shaking her head. "Tell me about it. Happens to me every time too."

"Is there something I can do for you? Has this happened to you before?" She really was looking rather pale.

"Unfortunately yes. I ran out of the house today without eating breakfast. I'm diabetic. I should know by now that I can't do that." My mom was also diabetic, so I knew exactly what the woman was talking about. Luckily, I also knew what to do to help.

"Just sit right here, and I'll be right back. Is there someone you want to call to give you a ride home? Driving right now probably isn't the best idea." I set the basket and towels on the floor, keeping my wallet in my hand.

"I suppose I should call my son. He should be able to give me a ride," the woman said as she dug her phone out of her purse.

I left the woman to her phone call and headed to the candy aisle that I had been trying to ignore. I grabbed a bag of licorice, chips, and a diet soda and went to the checkout. The dollar store didn't actually offer a healthy selection, but this would do in a pinch. The woman just needed to get her blood sugars back up.

I grabbed my things after paying and headed back to the bench. I ripped open the bag and handed it to the woman. "Oh dear, you didn't have to buy that. I could have given you money."

"Don't worry about it. I hope if this happened to my mom there would be someone to help her if I wasn't around."

"Well, that's awfully nice of you. My names Ethel Birch by the way."

"It's nice to meet you, Ethel. I'm Meg Grain. I also got you some chips and soda." I popped opened the soda and handed it to Ethel.

"Oh thank you, honey. My son is on the way here, should be only five minutes. You can get going if you want to, you don't need to sit with an old woman," Ethel said as she ate a piece of candy and took a slug of soda.

"No problem. The only plans I had today was to take a nap before work tonight. Delaying my plans by ten minutes won't be a problem."

"Well, in that case, you can help me eat this licorice. It's my favorite, but I shouldn't eat this all by myself. Where do you work at?" Ethel asked as she offered the bag to me.

"The factory right outside of town. I work in the warehouse, second shift." I grabbed a piece and sat down on the floor. If I was going to wait for Ethel's son to show up, might as well be comfortable while I waited for him.

"Really? Never would have thought that. Figured you would have said a nurse or something like that. Seems like you would have to be tough to work in a warehouse, sounds like a man's job."

I laughed. "Honestly, Ethel that is not the first time I have heard that, and it probably won't be the last.

You definitely need a certain attitude to deal with those truckers walking through the door. I have an awesome co-worker, so he helps out when truckers have a problem with a woman loading their truck."

"Sounds like you give them hell. My Tim was a trucker before he passed. I know exactly what you are talking about." Ethel took another drink of her soda and set it on the bench next to her.

"Feeling better?"

"Surprisingly, yes. It's a wonder what a little candy can do. How much do I owe you?" Ethel asked as she reached for her purse by her feet.

"Don't worry about it. I'm just glad that I was here to help."

"Mom! Where are you?" Someone yelled from the front of the store.

"Oh good, Lo's here. You'll have to meet him." Ethel cupped her hands around her mouth and yelled to him she was in the back.

I started getting up off the floor and remembered I wasn't exactly as flexible as I use to be while struggling to get up.

"Ma, you ok?" I was halfway to standing with my butt in the air when his voice made me pause.

It sounded like the man was gurgling broken glass when he spoke. Raspy and *so* sexy. Those three words he spoke sent shocks to my core. Lord knows the last time I felt anything in my core.

"Yes, I'm fine. I forgot to eat breakfast this morning and started to get dizzy when Meg here was nice enough to help me out until you could get here." Ethel turned to me. "Lo, this is Meg, Meg this is Lo."

Oh lord.

I couldn't talk. The man standing in front of me was ... oh, lord. I couldn't even think of a word to describe him.

I looked him up and down, and I'm sure my mouth was hanging wide open. I took in his scuffed up motorcycle boots and faded, stained ripped jeans that hugged his thighs and made me want to ask the man to spin so I could see what those jeans were doing for his ass. I moved my eyes up to his t-shirt that was tight around his shoulders and chest and showed he worked out.

I couldn't remember the last time I worked out. Did walking to the mailbox count as exercise? Of course, I only remembered to get the mail about twice a week, so that probably didn't count.

His arms were covered in tattoos. I could see them peeking out from the collar of his shirt and could only imagine what he looked like with his shirt off. Tattoos were my ultimate addiction on a man. Even one tattoo added at least 10 points to a man's hotness. This guy was off the fucking charts.

My eyes locked with his after my fantastic voyage up his body, and I stopped breathing.

"Hey, Meg. See something you like, darlin'?" Lo rumbled at me with a smirk on his face.

Busted. I sucked air back into my lungs and tried to remember how to breathe.

Lo's eyes were the color of fresh cut grass, bright green. His hair was jet black and cut close to his head with a pair of kick ass aviators sitting on top of his head. He was golden tan and gorgeous. The man was sex on a stick. Plain and simple.

"Uh, hey," I choked out.

Lo's lips curved up into a grin, and I looked down to see if my panties fell off. The man had a panty-dropping smile, and he wasn't even smiling that big. I would have to take cover or risk fainting if he smiled any bigger.

"Thanks for looking after my ma for me. I'm glad I was in town today and not out on a run," Lo said.

Ok. Get it together Meg. You are a 36-year-old woman, and this man has rendered you speechless like a sixteen-year-old girl. I needed to say something.

"Say something," I blurted out. Good Lord did I really just say that. Lo quirked his eyebrow, and his smirk returned.

"Ugh, I mean no problem. I didn't really do that much. No problem." I looked at Ethel while Lo was smirking at me; Ethel had a full-blown smile on her face and was beaming at me.

"You were a life saver, Meg! I don't know what I would have done if you weren't here." Ethel looked at Lo and grinned even bigger. "You should have seen her, Lo. She knew just what to do to help me. I could have sworn she was a nurse the way she took charge. She's not, though, just has a good head on her shoulders and decided to help this old lady out."

"That's good, Ma. You got all your shit you need so we can get going? I got some stuff going on at the garage that I dropped to get over here fast."

I took that as my cue to leave and ripped my eyes off Lo and bent over to get my basket and paper towels.

"Yes son, that's my stuff right here. I just want to get Meg's number before she leaves."

"Why do you need my number?" I asked as I juggled my basket and towels.

Ethel grabbed her purse off the ground and started digging through it again. "Well, you won't let me pay you back for the snacks you got for me so I figured I could pay you back by inviting you over for dinner sometime. So what's your number, sweetheart?"

"I don't eat dinner," I blurted out. I was really going to have to have a talk with my brain and mouth when I got home. They needed to get their shit together and start working in unison so I wouldn't sound like such an idiot.

"You don't eat dinner? Please don't tell me you're on a diet." Lo said as he looked me up and down.

"No," I said. Lord knew I should be.

Lo and Ethel just stared at me.

"So, no, you don't eat dinner?" Lo asked again.

"Yes. I mean no, I'm not on a diet. Yes, I eat dinner. I just work at night, so I meant that I wouldn't be able to come to dinner." I looked at Lo and blushed about ten shades of red. "Why is this so hard?"

"What's hard, sweetheart? Can't remember your phone number? I can barely remember mine too. Don't worry about not being able to make it to dinner; I can have you over for lunch. You eat lunch right?" Ethel asked with a smirk on her face. Lo had a full-blown smile on his face, even his eyes were smiling at me. That smile ought to be illegal.

I could see where Lo got his looks from. With Lo and Ethel standing next to each other, I could totally see the resemblance. Especially when they were both smirking.

I had to get out of here. I'm normally the one with the one-liners and making everyone laugh, now I couldn't even put two words together.

"Lunch would be good." I rattled off my number, and Ethel jotted it down.

"Ok, sweetheart, I'll let you get your nap. I'll give you a call later, and we can figure out a day we can get together." Ethel shoved the pen and paper back in her bag and leaned into me for a hug.

I awkwardly hugged her back and patted her on the shoulder. "Sounds good. Have a good day Ethel. Uh, it was nice meeting you, Lo," I mumbled as my gaze wandered over Lo again.

"You too Meg. See you around," Lo replied.

I gave them both a jaunty wave and booked it to the checkout. Thankfully there wasn't a line, and I quickly made my escape to my car. I threw my things in the trunk and hopped in. I grabbed my phone out of my pocket, plugged it into the radio, and turned on my chill playlist, the soothing sounds of Fleetwood Mac filled the car.

Music was the one thing in my life that had gotten me through so much shit. Good or bad, there was always a song that I could play, and it would make everything better. Right now I just needed to unscramble my brain and get my bearings. Fleetwood Mac singing "Landslide" was helping.

I pulled out of the parking lot and headed home. All I needed was to forget about today. If Ethel called for lunch, I would say yes because she did remind me so much of mom, but I wasn't going to let Lo enter my thoughts anymore. A woman like me definitely did not register on his radar, he was better just forgotten.

When I was halfway home, I realized I forgot dog food and shampoo.

Shit.

======

Lo

I helped mom finish her shopping and loaded all her crap into the truck. I looked around the parking lot for Meg, hoping she hadn't left yet so I could get another look at her. As soon as I saw her ass waving in the air as she struggled to stand up, I knew I had to be inside her.

It took all my willpower to not get a hard-on as her eyes ran over my body. Fucking chick was smoking' hot and didn't even know it.

"Thanks for coming to get me, Lo," Ma said as she interrupted my thoughts about Meg.

"No problem, Ma. I'll get one of the guys to bring your car to you later. Make sure it's locked." Ma dug her keys out of her huge ass purse and beeped the locks. We both got into the shop truck, and I started it up.

"Sure was nice of that Meg to help out. I don't know what I would have done without her."

"Yup, definitely nice of her." I shifted the truck into drive, keeping my foot on the brake, knowing exactly where mom was headed with this.

"You should ask her out." All I could do was shake my head and laugh.

"Straight to the point huh, Ma?"

"I'm old, I can say what I want. Meg is just the thing you need."

"I didn't know I needed anything." I pulled out of the parking lot and headed to Ma's house.

"You need someone in your life besides that club." My mom grabbed her phone out of her purse and started fiddling with it.

"We'll see, ma. Meg didn't seem too thrilled with me." She definitely liked what she saw, but it was like she couldn't get away from me quick enough when she saw that Ma was going to be ok.

"Well, you are pretty intimidating, Lo. Thank goodness you didn't wear your cut."

My leather vest with my club rockers and patches was a part of me. "What the hell is wrong with my cut? If some bitch can't handle me in my cut, she sure as shit doesn't belong with me," I growled.

"Not what I meant Lo. That girl has been hurt, you can see it in her eyes. You'll have to be gentle with her."

My phone dinged. I dug it out of my pocket and saw my mom had texted me. "You texted me her number, ma?"

"Use it, Logan, fix her," she insisted.

I sighed and pulled into mom's driveway. "Maybe she doesn't want to be fixed, ma. Maybe she has a boyfriend."

"She doesn't. Call her, or I'll do it for you," she ordered.

I knew my mom's threat wasn't idle. She totally would call Meg and ask her out for me. Fuck. "I'll help you get your shit inside ma."

"I'll make you lunch, and then you can call Meg," Ma said, as she jumped out of the truck and grabbed some bags.

I watched her walk into her house and looked at the message she had sent me. I saved Meg's number to my phone and grabbed the rest of Ma's shit and headed into the house.

Looked like I was calling Meg.

Grab Loving Lo.

Made in the USA
Monee, IL
11 July 2020